Samuel Milton Vernon

The Prohibition of the Liquor Traffic

Samuel Milton Vernon

The Prohibition of the Liquor Traffic

ISBN/EAN: 9783742899842

Manufactured in Europe, USA, Canada, Australia, Japa

Cover: Foto ©Andreas Hilbeck / pixelio.de

Manufactured and distributed by brebook publishing software
(www.brebook.com)

Samuel Milton Vernon

The Prohibition of the Liquor Traffic

THE

PROHIBITION

OF THE

LIQUOR TRAFFIC.

BY REV. S. M. VERNON, D. D..

Author of "Amusements," "Prohibition and Punishment," Etc.

P. W. ZIEGLER & CO.,

PHILADELPHIA AND CHICAGO,

1888.

TO

MY BROTHER
HON. J. W. VERNON

THIS VOLUME IS

AFFECTIONATELY DEDICATED.

PREFACE.

THERE is little need for a preface to a book like this. The nature of the subject and the form of treatment make it easy for the average reader to comprehend it without the aid of note or comment. The real preface was written long ago by God's avenging natural laws in a record of suffering and death, with which all are familiar. It is God's protest against man's sin, announced in the form of the evils which like a devouring conflagration follow in the track of intemperance. If men would stop to consider what God has thus said in tones that fill the whole land with lamentation, there would be little need for my poor speech on this subject. In its presence any human speech is insipid and spiritless. There is in it the sweep of Divine thought, the throb of infinite tenderness and the majesty of supreme authority. The most to which I aspire in this volume is to translate this handwriting of God into language all can understand, and to point the way of escape from the evils it portrays. If at my voice men will pause to hear what God and eternal truth, as revealed in nature and man's constitution, are saying about the evils of intemperance, I shall have accomplished the greatest possible service to my race.

If my neighbor were drowning, I should not feel it necessary to declare or defend my motives in trying to save him. Neither do I feel called upon to give other account of the appearance of this book than that I saw the people perishing, and lifted up my voice to warn them, to call for help and to point out the way of escape. I may indeed confess that while doing this as best I could in other ways, it was the invitation of my kind publishers to write for them, that gave my voice the form it now takes in this publication. Man's brotherhood to man requires that by all possible means he shall seek to lift off the burdens that oppress the race, suppress the vices that corrupt it, put out the fires that are consuming it, and direct others to the paths of peace which his own feet have found. To remove the greatest cause of sorrow in the home, of dishonor to manhood, of demoralization to childhood and youth, and of heart-breaking anguish to woman, is a work so grand as to make one shrink away in conscious unworthiness, and yet to which one is bound by every feeling of loyalty to humanity and to God.

If no one should heed my voice, I shall at least have the consolation, so sweet to all toilers for God and the suffering race, of having done what I could. I also indulge the hope that by God's blessing on the word here spoken, it may hasten the day when strong drink being banished from our midst, " there shall be nothing to hurt or to harm in all the holy mountain of God."

S. M. VERNON.

CONTENTS.

CHAPTER I.

STATEMENT.

CHAPTER II.

SCIENTIFIC DEMONSTRATION.

CHAPTER III.

COMMON SENSE.

CHAPTER IV.

LOGIC.

CHAPTER V.

MORAL RIGHT.

measure they have meted it shall be measured to them again If these men were ignorant of the results of their business they might be excused, but they know it all. Many of them deplore the results, but see the money in it and will have it. Some of them boast over the number of barrels of whiskey they sell, and chuckle over the fights that will come out of them. They haved loved cursing and cursing shall be the portion of their cup. The saloon keeper and the criminal stand on the same footing. No one disputes the moral right of seizing the tools and booty of the train robber.   Page 47.

CHAPTER VI.

LEGAL RIGHT.

CHAPTER VII.

INDIVIDUAL RIGHTS.

CHAPTER VIII.

REFORMATION BY LAW.

as the church. It is necessary to the church. Law a great educator, and a
rule for the development of character. It restrains the evil and stimulates
the good in human nature. It also affords security to society. It is objected
that a prohibitory law could not be enforced, and therefore would be demoralizing. The truth to be proclaimed whether men will regard it or not.
Page 83.

CHAPTER IX.

MORAL AND LEGAL SUASION.

All agree to moral suasion. Legal suasion objected to by liquor dealers,
but demanded in the interests of reform. Prohibition would give moral suasion a chance. It would at once stop casual drinking. Would protect the
10,000,000 boys now in peril. It would make drinking disreputable by making
it necessary to consort with law-breakers in order to drink. It would give us
protection for our property and persons. We go to sleep now every night
with dynamite in the cellar. All in peril while the saloon exists. Page 90.

CHAPTER X.

CHARACTER.

The character of the liquor traffic justifies its prohibition. It is a law-
breaker. It corrupts the sources of law. It bribes voters, legislatures and
courts. It is a thief, taking from the people $1,000,000,000 annually, and giving
only cursing in return. It does this in the first case by deception, then by
force. It is a murderer, taking the life of the drinker, and making him the
destroyer of other lives. 100,000 die annually from effects of strong drink.
It is a co-partner with all vices and crimes. The saloon a school of vice, the
vicious classes move about it as a common center. Men show character by
their business and associations. Wholesale dealers no better than retailers.
Page 97.

CHAPTER XI.

WILL IT PROHIBIT?

License laws fail. Taxing does not restrain. All the saloon asks is the
privilege to live. Liquor dealers object to prohibition because it will be a
failure. Hypocrites! The devil as an angel of light. The enemy's weak
point. Uncle Ben's logic. Both sides recognize prohibition as effective.
Testimony to facts sustained by success of prohibition in Maine, Gov.
Dingley, Gov. Perham, Hon. W. P. Frye, Hon. Lat M. Morrill, Hon.
Hannibal Hamlin, Hon. J. G. Blaine. Hon. John Lynch, Hon. Jas. A.
Peters, Hon. Eugene Hale, Hon. Woodbury Davis, Horace Greeley, Hon.
Benj. Kingsbury, J. H. Drummond, J. S. Wheelwright, Hon. Joshua
Nye. Hon. Neal Dow. George William Curtis. Dr. R. Locke. Kansas a prohi-
bition State. Law well enforced. *Independence Tribune, Parsons Star,
Kansas Methodist.* H. Winfield Brewer, James H. Troutman, *Augusta Repub-
lican,*Gov. John H. Martin. *Toledo Blade,*Hon. S. B. Bradford, Iowa adopted pro-
hibition. Gov. Sherman testifies to its success. Fifty editors, *Toledo Blade,*
Hector Ballendon, Rev. M. Bamford. Senator Clark's bill for enforcement.
Des Moines *State Register.* The Dubuque *Prohibitionist.* Jails empty.
Local option. Prohibition in Atlanta. *Atlanta Constitution.* Senator Col-
quitt. Dr. H. C. Haygood. Dr. J. B. Hawthorne. Grand Jury. Savannah
News. Education for prohibition going on. Page 115.

CHAPTER XII.

POLITICS.

The temperance question an unwelcome intruder in the political arena.
Politics need a disturbing element. The discussion of great moral questions
elevates and purifies. The last twenty years no great discussions of living
ideas in political world. Great questions have been crowded out, politicians
busy with party interests. Chinese, Mormon, Negro questions, treated to high-
sounding platitudes capable of different interpretations. Supreme effort in
politics to secure and hold office. The exclusion of great moral questions

CHAPTER XIII.

OUR FORCES.

CHAPTER XIV.

CONCLUSION.

CHAPTER I.

GOD has but one method with evil, he prohibits it. He makes no compromises with it, has no system of fees, taxes, or penalties, upon the payment of which it may be allowed; but everywhere meets it with a definite and peremptory "thou shalt not," which admits of no bartering and no appeal. The device of licensing it upon the payment of a price, is one of those "inventions" by which men proclaim their alienation from God, and place themselves under his displeasure. As it is not possible for God "to look upon iniquity," save to condemn it, so it is not possible for any of his subjects, while loyal to him, to declare a thing legal which he pronounces illegal. He who approves and tolerates what God condemns, puts himself at war with God. If this toleration is procured by the payment of a price, the alienation and demoralization are all the greater. The back turned upon the Master, and the hand reached out for the thirty pieces of silver, has too long been the attitude of the world in relation to the liquor traffic. All this license mongering is a confession of guilt at this point, for the fee is exacted and received on the theory that the traffic is a monstrous iniquity that ought not to exist, but which, in our goodness, we allow to continue on condition of the price paid.

Everyone can see that the principle could not be maintained in the Divine government, where we expect absolute holiness. If God were to fix a scale of prices

9

for exemption from the commands of the decalogue, every one would feel that henceforth God and devil were synonymous terms. The idea is admissible at all only when we adopt the theory of the prince of darkness, that the Divine government is not to be accepted as an example for man's imitation.

As matter of fact, however, human governments have, in theory at least, accepted the Divine law as their guide. It has been the boast of our modern civilization, that the word of God is the corner-stone of its magnificent superstructure. Severe prohibitory laws have been enacted against the great crimes condemned by Divine revelation. To license murder, theft, piracy, or treason, has never entered into the minds of our astute statesmen, who seem to find abundant reason for licensing that which is known to produce four-fifths of all the crimes and miseries that now oppress society. Government has accepted the principle of the prohibition of evil, but our statesmen have been outwitted by the ministers of evil and have consented to forbid the thing, but to allow its chief cause to remain in full force. No man is willing to pay or receive a tax for murder, but our enlightened christian governments are in the humiliating position of levying taxes for the right of existence upon that which makes men murderers. This solecism is, it may be, due to a want of careful thought, or it may be to the blinding effect of the large financial interests both to the individual engaged in the traffic and to the government.

The present great popular movement towards prohibition, by which several states have been lifted into the sunlight of a more perfect freedom than has been known on this continent, is the result of growing intelligence, and an awakening of conscience among the people. We could ask nothing more for the triumph of our cause than that the people will observe, read and think about it. Clear, earnest thinking points inevitably away from the saloon and towards prohibition. This is the burning question in social political and ecclesiastical circles, "what shall we do with the liquor traffic?" In this, is our hope, that the people will not stop thinking about the question, for if they think long enough for their thoughts to crystalize into actions, and deep enough to get to foundation principles and bottom facts, the fate of the liquor traffic is sealed.

And, indeed, "our friends the enemy," are very helpful to us at this point. They have assumed the aggressive. They have dictated to our legislative bodies license laws, drawn in the interests of the traffic, only to break and trample them under their feet, with derision and bold defiance. They have formed vast organizations with the avowed intention of controlling or resisting legislation. They have poured out immense sums of money to corrupt voters, and to bribe legislatures. They have procured the assassination of earnest opponents of this destructive traffic, and contributed liberally of their money to defend the instruments of their malice. They fill our homes with lamentation, our streets with disorder, our jails with criminals, and our alms houses with paupers. The crape on the door is the black flag of the traffic, which has startled the nation into a realization of the nature of the conflict. If we would let the rum traffic alone, it will not let us alone. If we say, "peace, peace," and sit down to enjoy quiet, the next day the monster will boldly march through the street with the idol of our homes between his blood-stained jaws. The people at last begin to see that the question is, to kill or to be killed, and their grave earnest discussions indicate their purpose of brave self-defense. The mists have lifted a little, the people are looking about to discover the true state of the case, and the general result is a deep conviction that as the forces now stand, it is the saloon against the home, the school, the state, and the church, with the spirit of murder well developed on one side, and the spirit of prohibition rapidly rising on the other. This is American thought to-day on this subject.

This hoary monster, the liquor traffic, stands arraigned at the bar of the public conscience, charged with a countless number of murders, rapes, suicides and riots, and sixty millions of people are invited to pronounce whether he shall be led forth to execution or be released to continue his work. Humanity itself stands waiting a verdict that will avenge or sanction the wrongs of the past, that will protect or lay waste the unborn generations of the future. If a Bengal tiger were prowling through our streets who would need argument or entreaty for his instant death? The sight of one mangled human body would silence all questions about probable financial loss to the owner. A thousand such wild beasts are to-day, as simple matter of fact, if we will open our eyes to see it, lurking about the street corners of American cities, waiting an opportunity to spring upon the husband and father as he goes to his daily toil, to seize and fatten upon the school boys who go to their duties with their mother's kiss upon their brow, or to drink the life blood of the unfortunate wife and mother who endeavors in vain to protect the idol of her home from the destroyer. Upon these monsters, whose real character and work can have escaped only the thoughtless or the wilfully blind, we ask the boasted intelligence, patriotism and moral courage of this enlightened age to pronounce its considerate judgment.

I unhesitatingly declare for condemnation, and ask your patience in considering what seem to me good and sufficient reasons for it, in the hope that I may carry conviction to your mind, secure the compliment of your agreement with my opinions, and enlist for the cause of prohibition another loyal defender. If our investigation is to be real and of value, we must take firm hold upon the truth; look stern facts lovingly in the face till we learn their deepest meaning; open the windows of our souls toward eternal realities and admit their full light; walk with unfaltering step where inexorable logic leads; obey the voice of conscience, accept the verdict of reason, and bow in loyal submission to the demands of the highest good. Let us put away prejudice, wave all fanatics aside, ask enthusiasts for once to be silent, drive out blear-eyed appetite, and bid hideous old avarice wait outside the door; while with telegraphic connections with every breaking heart, every ruined home, every watching, praying mother and wife, every bloated victim of the destroyer's poison, and every soul in hell sent thither by strong drink we proceed in the presence of the "Judge of the whole earth," and with the eyes of all men on us, to render a just decision of the question whether this traffic shall live or die.

Before proceeding to a formal consideration of the question, look at this hideous monster a moment. These locks, whitened by the frosts of three thousand years, are matted with blood and filth; his bleared eyes have in their depths only the light of craft, lust and murder; his bloated face suggests only coarse brutality, base indulgences and fiendish cruelties; his defiled rai-

ment shows that he has been wallowing in the street and
consorting with all vile things that creep and crawl;
and his blood-stained hands declare him to have been a
common, unrestrained murderer. Ask those standing
about—yea, ask the whole world, if any one has any
good to allege of him? What page of history has he
adorned with the record of noble deeds? What virtues
has he maintained in himself or developed in others?
What arts or industries has he fostered for the good of
society? Where has there been an evil with which he
has not sought an alliance, and where an effort for the
uplifting of mankind that has not found in him a deadly
foe? Where are the statistics of the charities he has
sustained, the missions he has established, the moral
reforms he has inaugurated, the communities improved
in intelligence, domestic happiness and moral excellence
by his presence, and of the individual lives he has
brightened and blessed? Can anything be said in
defense of his right to live, save that he ministers to the
appetites and avarice of depraved men? Where has he
ever furnished bread for the table, clothing for the body,
tools for the hands, intelligence for the mind, or moral
excellence for the soul? Do not all men look on him
with horror? Do not the widows and orphans of the
land cry night and day to heaven for vengeance on his
guilty head?

The proposition now pending before the American
people, awaiting their consideration and their suffrages,
is that this monster shall be driven from the street and
forbidden to return to its deadly work. It is a question of such magnitude, so related to vast financial,
social, educational and religious interests, that the brain
wearies in the attempt to grasp its full meaning. No

civilized people ever sat in solemn judgment on a greater question, measuring its greatness by the cold yard stick of unsentimental statistics. Raising only the questions considered by unsentimental statesmen and social philosophers, touching finance, public health, social order, domestic quiet and happiness, and the stability of the state, the subject becomes immeasurably greater than all others before the American people. Daniel Webster, Henry Clay, nor Patrick Henry, ever had such a cause to plead, and if their eloquence and courage are not equaled, it will be because their posterity has fallen into intellectual and moral decay. Apathy on this subject must arise either from intellectual stupidity, or moral effeminacy. To the intellectual giant it affords a rare opportunity, from the standpoint of the financier, the statesman, the humanitarian, the moralist and the religionist, it spreads far and wide, and rises "Alp on Alp," snow-capped and gleaming, till the mind is bewildered with its vastness and grandeur. Genius never stood before a more enchanting prospect, and loyal devotion to man and God never had a better field; while the prince of darkness never stood forth to the conflict with his own proper character so clearly manifested, and in league with an ally so well designed to aid his purposes. The midnight brawl, pistol shot, and cry of murder, the spreading conflagration and surging riot, the haggard mothers and ragged children, the reeling men and besotted women, the crape on the door and the voice of lamentation in the street, reveal the presence of the destroyer and summon us to the work of rescue.

CHAPTER II.

SCIENTIFIC DEMONSTRATION.

CONCEDING that the evil exists as alleged and that it ought to be cured, the question still remains "is prohibition the true cure?" It is assumed in these pages that it is the best and the only cure for the form in which it exists in this country. We are not concerned about the drinking habits of a people who lived six thousand miles from our shores, in a climate and an age very different from ours, of which faint glimpses are given in the Bible. From the days of Noah, who appears in an unenviable plight in its use, "wine has been a mocker," though we freely grant that its work has been much less destructive under some circumstances than under others. Neither are we concerned about the drinking customs of some European countries said to be so harmless. They do not exist with us, and have no relation to the present discussion, except to point a suggestive contrast. If we succeed in rooting up our present diabolical drinking customs, it will then be time to raise the question whether the wine drinking habits of France and Italy, or the beer drinking habits of Germany, could be wisely transferred to this country. We need no word of written revelation on this subject, since God is giving us a new one every day, written on our very paving stones, on the walls that rise either side of the street, and in letters of blood across the page of all contemporary history. He who will not be persuaded by this, would not be though one rose from the dead to declare it. Our business is to hold the American saloon up in the light and look at it; to let the light shine through it, revealing all that is within; to study it; to find out what it is doing, what its relation is to physical health, financial prosperity and morality; and on the discovered facts to dispose of it as they require. .

We do not invite the enemy to an easy victory by taking the position that in itself wine drinking is a sin. This is the baldest assumption with no support from scripture or logic. The doctrine of prohibition needs no forced interpretation of scripture, no pious sentimental cant. It asks only for cool, clear, honest thinking, for a fair interpretation of the facts of experience, and for an unprejudiced judgment upon current events known to everyone. If it rests on fanaticism and sentiment; if its necessity can not be demonstrated in a strictly scientific way; if it does not reckon with all the facts of human experience in an impartial way; if it is not in harmony with the common instincts and impulses of humanity; then let us put a mill-stone about its neck and sink it a hundred fathoms deep in the sea.

The doctrine of prohibition is capable of scientific demonstration. The scientific method is to collect facts without reference to theory. Collect from as large a field as possible, and when you have your facts, put them together, classify them, and accept as theory what they agree in making necessary. Our facts are collected from three thousand years of human history in all the habitable lands of the globe, a vast field affording abundant material. The facts have been dug up from every mine that was ever opened, they have waved on high their significance in every field of golden grain swayed by July's ripening winds, they have been borne aloft in

2

the street parades of all cities, and have been washed up along the shores of all seas.

Let us go back to the morning of history, and suppose one of our pure progenitors presented for the first time with three cups—one containing water, one milk and one wine, with the request to take his choice. Without experience or observation as to the effect of either, his choice would be without any moral quality, for he would not have the knowledge upon which to base an intelligent moral action. He would be just as good a man taking the wine as he would be taking the water. But it soon appears that the wine has an injurious effect, begets an abnormal appetite which leads to disastrous consequences, and pauses not in its deadly work till it has laid all in ruins. We are now forced by experience, the scientific method, to revise our judgment of the character of the first choice. We observe another pass through a like sad and bitter experience, and the terrible work of the wine cup becomes more and more manifest. Fact on fact of horrid mein rises before us to convince our reluctant judgments, till no room for doubt is left. Finding others in the process of experimenting with the destroyer, we hasten to inform them of the results of our observations, and are amazed to find that argument is powerless before confirmed habit. The appetite spreads through the community like an infection, and stronger drinks are brought in to give the effects no longer obtained from the light wines. The evils increase, diseased bodies, unbalanced minds, debased moral natures, disordered social relations, waste of substance, shame, dishonor and premature death, all appear as legitimate consequences. We are filled with horror at the spectacle, and finding the results the same in a wide field of observation in different ages and nationalities, we reverse our judgment about the innocence of the wine cup, and even go so far as to say that it ought not to be placed before men to tempt their choice.

But we are informed that men should not go to these excesses, that the evil is in the excess. This seems reasonable, so we begin to warn men against excess. We point out the dangers and enlarge upon the evils of intemperance, but to our horror, find that Laocoon was not more helpless with the serpents wrapped about his limbs and body, than are many of these victims of an appetite acquired by moderate drinking. The effort is continued century after century, with the same heart-sickening result, and again, in the most rigid scientific way we find that the cry against excess is one of the siren songs that lures to destruction, and that the first glass is a very "Circes' cup" which transforms a man into a beast. The facts lie open to view over all the page of history, and whoever will may walk out, and in half an hour pick up skulls enough to convince him that this is a very "death trap."

Over this rout of argument and experience the race has come in a mournful procession, endeavoring to restrain its growing convictions, conceal its defeats, and hide from the public eye its incomparable losses, till now, weary of its unsuccessful effort, by a mighty rebound, it is giving conscience a voice that is shaking the nations. A countless number of lives have been sacrificed in the process of discovering the true nature of strong drink, but now that there is little doubt left on this point among intelligent people, it will require a shrewder serpent than the one that prevailed against our first parents to induce the race to tolerate this destroyer,

But in this scientific method of investigating the rum evil, another class of facts comes to view, throwing a strong light on the question of prohibition. Back of the maddened, crazed multitudes that are rushing upon destruction, we find a large class of men with capital invested in the manufacture and sale of what we are endeavoring to keep from these men. They expose it for sale in attractive places and in ways to enlist the passions and stimulate the appetites, and by various devices seek to break down the consciences and self command of their victims. Long and bitter experience teaches that the weakness of human nature and the power of the charmer are such, that if strong drink is exposed for sale, there will always be a considerable number who will fall under its power. From the days of Noah, history has lifted up its warning voice, and slow as men have been to learn the unwelcome truth in the presence of a loud outcry about the power of the human will and the sacredness of personal liberty as to what one shall eat and drink, it is now generally recognized by thoughtful people that the incoming of the drinking saloon in a community means demoralization, waste and death.

To expose strong drink for sale is a seed sowing for a harvest of drunkards that may be depended upon with certainty, and may be estimated with a good degree of accuracy from the character of the soil, and the amount of skill and labor to be employed in its cultivation. With this experience to guide us, a logical mind at once asks: "Is it not then the quickest way to end this work of destruction to prohibit the business? If there are no liquors sold there can be none bought. To make an end of drinking, make it impossible to buy. To stop buying, prohibit selling." This prohibition logic is plain, simple and irrefutable, and let those who think it visionary and impracticable reserve their judgment till we come to treat that phase of the subject, which will not be found wanting in the support of the soundest of arguments.

To all this, however, it is replied that no man is compelled to buy what is offered for sale, and, therefore, those who buy, do so by their own choice, and are alone responsible for their acts and the consequences that may follow. That they are alone responsible does not appear, for if the article had not been offered for sale, it would not have been bought, and the two parties are partners in guilt as they are associates in the transaction. The article was exposed for sale, with a distinct knowledge of its character and effects, and with the hope that there would be those whose appetites would be so stimulated by its presence, as to make them regardless of consequences, and thus afford the profits for which the traffic was undertaken. The business is projected upon a shrewd calculation of human weakness, upon the overmastering powers of appetite and passion, upon the sure support and co-operation of all the vices that infest society, and is in its deepest thought and secret purpose criminal and murderous, and is, therefore, to be expelled from society. It calculates upon success by taking the wages, the health, the home comforts, and finally the life of the laboring man ; by enticing the school boy, whom it turns out of school, then out of good society, then out of home, then into the gutter, then into the grave ; by poisoning the blood of the father till his brain is crazed, and he becomes in the home a demon and a murderer, to be executed to satisfy the public conscience, and by laying waste everything held dear in human society. It seems like mocking the common sense of mankind to ask for the considerate judgment of enlightened men upon such a traffic.

It is frankly conceded that men ought to have more self-control, that they ought not to run to these excesses, but we are now considering the facts of experience and asking what light do they throw upon this great question of the liquor traffic. We find that as matter of fact men have not this self-control, and that to preach it while holding out to them a glass of wine is little better than to insist upon self-control in a mass of gunpowder while applying a lighted match to it. We have been experimenting at great cost, and find that wherever we put down a drinking saloon, infection begins and spreads through the community with no determinable limits. Not the intellectual imbecile and social outcast only, but all classes, the highest as well as the lowest, are put in peril. How the flames seem to delight to climb, hiss and roar among the grand arches, along the magnificent aisles and far reaching rafters, and up the cloud piercing spires of these royal natures, whose very greatness often seems to render them specially liable to burst into conflagration! The "honor man" of his class just from college, the bright young physician, the aspiring politician, the successful merchant, the promising lawyer, and even the holy sanctuary itself is invaded, and the minister of religion falls a prey to the charms of the destroyer. There is no home in the community where the dram shop exists from which, the only son may not be carried forth to a drunkard's grave, or the only daughter, in becoming a drunkard's wife, be consigned to a living death so terrible that no pen can paint its horrors. Bitter experience, a wise, stern old teacher, has a thousand lectures with glowing periods, delivered with thundering intonations, illustrated by maps and charts covering a period of three thousand years, in which he demonstrates to all who will give attention, that there is no safety in the vicinity of the dram shop, and that the only wise course is to banish it from the earth. Whichever way we turn, the terrible facts of experience glare down upon us, warning us of the dangers lurking in the saloon, crying out to us for vengeance on it as the mother of abominations, and pleading with us for a decree of total prohibition against it. It is impossible to treat the subject with scientific fairness and thoroughness without conceding the justness of this claim.

CHAPTER III.

COMMON SENSE.

NATURAL instinct and common sense, no less than scientific research, sustain the claims of prohibition. Not only do the facts of history justify it, but the common impulses and judgments of humanity in the lowest tribes as well as in the most civilized nations sustain it. The common sentiment of men everywhere has been that whatever proves itself destructive or highly injurious to society ought to be cast out. In its struggle for self-preservation and for progress from the savage to the civilized state, certain instincts and ruling propensities always appear, and are recognized as essential in human nature and human progress. Among these none have been more pronounced than that named above, which has been one of the guiding lights of the race, "the pillar of cloud and fire" in the wilderness of time, by which man has made progress toward his promised Canaan. Our theory of prohibition has in it nothing of fanaticism or rashness, but is simply the advance guard of the mighty host, that for thousands of years has been pushing forward along the lines of instinct, guided by common sense, with a discipline knit as tight as logic could make it, in obedience to conscience, having come at last where it may dip its feet into the waters of the Jordan, and taste a little of the fruits of that. "good land" just before it.

To go back upon the track of history to the lowest point, and study the beginnings of human progress, will reveal the wide sweep and the mighty force of this principle. By what processes of reasoning, and on what principles did man come to take his position toward the animals which at the first he found as neighbors in this world? Bring before an uninstructed man, all the animals in the world, and he would probably choose a tiger before a cow and a lion before a donkey. But after a little experience he would ask the privilege of revising his choice. He would soon decide to send away the lion and tiger, but to his horror might find that they were not disposed to go, and that he must either kill them or change his place of abode, if so fortunate as to gain their permission to do so. He would also find that the donkey and the cow had capacities for service that did not at first appear. The attitude of civilized men to-day toward these animals in every part of the world presupposes such an experience as this, is accounted for by it, and there is not a people on the face of the earth, civilized or savage, so stupid as to insist upon ignoring this experience, and proving for itself whether the tiger or the donkey is the more amiable and servicable. Why do men prohibit the whole brood of serpents, wild beasts, destructive poisonous insects, and all parasites, and arm themselves for their destruction wherever they may find them? Why is it considered not only lawful, but a duty to mankind to kill any of the prohibited classes wherever found at large? Why, but because by experience it has been found that wherever they roam abroad human life is unsafe? The wild beast which a man sees in the forest may be fleeing from him, or the man may be in a safe position out of danger, yet the human conscience everywhere declares that he ought to shoot it, lest happening upon some other person in less fortunate circumstances, it might use its opportunities, or at least that one of its cubs might at some time in the future chance to meet a defenseless human being and demonstrate its power over him. Travel to the utmost limits of the race, and you will find in the lowest tribes this settled conviction of duty and this unalterable practice, founded upon and justified by human experience. There the passions and appetites are not largely interested, conscience and reason have acted with but little obstruction, and absolute prohibition has been declared and is well executed against destroyers not so much to be feared as the blood-thirsty monster against which we are endeavoring to arouse the public conscience. Wherever men are in the neighborhood of wild beasts to-day, in the jungles of India, in the wilds of Africa, or in the mountains of Colorado, there is absolute unanimity in their approval and execution of the rule adopted by mankind with reference to them. No company of men could be found so ignorant of the powers of prevailing public opinion on this subject as to propose to open in one of our large cities a menagerie, with the privilege of allowing their animals to roam the streets during certain hours of the day for the amusement and instruction of the people, who might view them with perfect safety from the windows of their upper stories, agreeing meanwhile to pay into the city treasury a heavy license fee as an offset for the damage inflicted in the occasional loss of a life by some reckless adventurer who did not keep within the safety line. Such a proposition would be laughed to scorn as the wildest vagary of a set of fanatics, and yet every large city in the land does maintain a destroying agent in its streets, worse than a menagerie with unlocked cage doors. Worse, because

more people are destroyed by it. Worse, because he has
the fearful power of begetting in his victim an appetite
corresponding to his own, so that he rushes into the
embrace of death as by his own choice. Worse, because
the death is so much more terrible. The young man
overtaken in the street and devoured by a wild beast,
would have the sympathy of his neighbors, would be
mourned by all, his virtues would be extolled, his friends
would console themselves by saying, "he brought no
reproach upon his father's house, he was an honor to his
mother, there is not a stain upon his character." The
young man who falls by the demon of strong drink, is
first deprived of his self-respect, his will instead of being
a king is made a slave, his conscience is outraged, and
every good quality in him is cast into the dust; then his
reputation is blackened and he made the subject of
ridicule in the street among base men and lewd women:
then the community is turned against him as one who has
dishonored it and the race, his own friends cover their
faces for shame and mourn for him more than for one
dead; then, and not till then, after a thousand deaths
have been inflicted, does the fatal blow fall. The wild
beast is merciful and tender in comparison with this
monster, which our boasted civilization by its arts has
conjured up from the bottomless pit. There is not a
man civilized or savage so deficient in instinct and
natural reason as to attempt to live in the vicinity of
wild beasts, unless he can put upon them the absolute
prohibition of iron bars or stone walls. The daring
hunter never so far loses his reason as to gratify the
wish of his children, by tying a beautiful panther about
the neck to a tree in his door yard, with a rope which may
snap at one bound, leaving all at the mercy of the blood-

thirsty monster. Such folly is left for his more enlightened brother of our highly cultivated communities, whose natural instincts have been somewhat blunted by spacious theories about personal liberty and the right of unrestrained traffic, till he confidingly allows the saloon in his very door yard with only the slender cord of a license law about its neck.

There was a time when man had to choose between poison and healthful food for his table, whether by Divine instruction, or by experience, he came to a knowledge of poisons, and promptly excluded them from his table, and upon this decision the race continues to act with practical unanimity. If one now insists upon ignoring this prohibition enacted and enforced by common consent, and insists upon a new demonstration in his own person or household, he is adjudged either criminal or insane.

The history of human legislation is a history of the prohibition of vices and assumed personal rights. The decalogue begins with "thou shalt not," and our modern legislation concerns itself chiefly with re-echoing the Divine prohibition, translating it into the speech of our times, and adapting it to present customs. Not only are human vices forbidden, but also whatever is found to be injurious or dangerous to society. Upon all grades and forms of life society uses with relentless vigor the prohibition pruning hook. If a man buys a lot in a part of the city where great buildings contain valuable stores, he is prohibited from erecting on it a wooden building, though it were to be devoted to the sacred services of religion, or the care of the sick and dying, because the liability of wooden structures to burn would put the surrounding valuable property in peril. A man may own his own business block and bring into it dry goods, groceries, hardware or what he will, but if he attempts to store gunpowder in his cellar, society will prohibit it, because it has been found that gunpowder will sometimes explode to the destruction of surrounding property. A man may buy a beautiful tract on both sides of a stream, and proceed to erect a mill and construct a dam, but if society concludes that the back water will make the neighborhood unhealthy it will prohibit the dam. A man may bring from the ends of the earth, at great cost, the fastest horse that ever lifted hoof, but society will prohibit the trial of his speed in the park or street, because it has been found that in such places fast driving endangers the lives of other parties. A man may, for the good of society and for his own profit, establish a soap factory in a populous part of the city, but if the odors become offensive the factory will be prohibited. Vegetables and meats, the results of hard and honest toil, may be brought to the market, but their sale is strictly prohibited, except in certain conditions.

The common sense of mankind has carried it into every department of life, and now seeks to apply it to the most obnoxious case of all, the saloon. If so, in accord with the common practice of society, it may be asked, why has not this policy been applied here, where there is most need for it? What strange spell has this one deadly foe to human interests thrown over society? How has it palsied the active brain? By what power has it stifled the consciences of the most devout men? What arts has it used to betray sharp-eyed instinct? How has it been able to cozen society and make it believe that wholesale murder was but the effervescence of innocent pleasure-seeking? Who can account for the prevailing apathy on this subject? Why do people sleep securely with this volcano belching sulphurous fire at their very door-steps? Why do christians read the appalling record of each day's destruction and do nothing? Do they not care that the people are destroyed, that crime and death go hand in hand, lashed by this demon, through all our streets? There is not a more discouraging spectacle to the philosophical philanthropist than the apathy and indifference of the general public to the desolation of the liquor traffic. A hundred savages turned loose with a government commission to gratify without restraint their passion for murder and torture, would not give us such a daily record of horrors as are afforded by this traffic, and yet the intelligent public allows no decisive interference. We cannot understand the case without considering this feature of it carefully. The gravity of the situation is in the fact that society at large, as well as the individual victim of strong drink, is narcotized beyond the point of acting with intelligent judgment and conscientious integrity. Men of high moral character as individuals have basely consented to allow society to be debauched, the young corrupted, and every interest of the community put in peril; to hold their speech, while murder and riot are being hatched in the cocatrice den across the street. We shall never understand the liquor problem unless we remember that the song of the siren is in the air, and that society at large has been strangely transformed by it. The old Greek dreamers saw the truth clearly, and their Cerce was a terrible reality, and so is ours. We shall never escape this charm till our Ulysses crew of prohibitionists become devoted, and strong enough to lash themselves fast to their masts for life or death, and then lift up their voices in songs, louder and sweeter than those of the Siren.

The public, now half awakened, has, up to this time, failed to pronounce sentence upon the disturber of its peace, because Satan came to it disguised as an angel of light, and thus deceived it. He introduced himself as the source of "innocent pleasure," and as all men feel that they have more trouble than justly belongs to them, and that it is their right to balance the accounts by a little indulgence, this claim met with eager acceptance. When once the trial was made the poison generated rapidly enough to inflame the passions and cloud the understanding sufficiently to hold the victim in its grasp. It claimed to be heaven's appointed stimulant for overtaxed physical and mental energies, and as all men feel that they are overtaxed in one or the other of these ways there was in this claim a powerful appeal to human weakness; the falseness of which was not discovered till the unfortunate victim was too far gone to care anything about it. It claimed to be the inspiring genius of social good cheer, and thus gained admission to and finally captured society, which it has enslaved and degraded. It was found a powerful ally of business success, for after a stimulating glass, trade and traffic ran smoother, and when business was done the customer expected the courtesy of a parting glass as a pledge of future patronage. Back of all these and other influences was the enormous profit of the liquor dealer, as a powerful stimulus to him to push his trade into every nook and corner of society, and hold it there at all cost. With all these influences at work, pulling with the current of depraved human nature, it is not strange that the promptness of society to prohibit evil in other forms should not here appear. But because slow and long suffering, it will be all the more resolute when fully aroused and disenchanted.

CHAPTER IV.

LOGIC.

NO cause ever had a better support in sound argument than that which we are advocating. If it were possible to put aside all sentiment, to shut out the cry of distress that goes up to God night and day, to suppress every feeling of commiseration, to close our eyes to all moral considerations, and as cold logicians, look at the bare facts as they stand out on the surface of society, we should find arguments like mountain ranges, "piled Alp on Alp" to the very skies. The logic of prohibition is like the chain lightning of heaven, nothing can stand before it. So vast and overwhelming are the simple facts that the mind can with difficulty handle them. No cause advocated among men, aside from religion, has a basis of fact and argument to compare with the cause of prohibition. It concerns every nation, every human interest, and recites a catalogue of wrongs, compared with which that contained in the declaration of American independence, or in any other document promulgated against tyranny and oppression in behalf of an oppressed or an enslaved people, seems utterly trivial and contemptible. We ask nothing in behalf of party, creed, or sickly moral sentiment, but we do ask that the full light of reason may be turned upon the cold facts of this case, and that a verdict be rendered according to the facts. There is nothing the hosts of darkness have to fear so much as the terrible logic of this question. Make the people see and understand the facts, and the traffic will have but a short lease of life on these shores. It would be amusing if it were not so diabolical, to see these bloated, befouled monsters who keep alive the fires of hell on earth, put their heads up out of their dens and shout "fanaticism! fanaticism!" This cry will influence no man who understands its source and inspiration. Too often we have responded with invective and coarse abuse, while Heaven's artillery was shotted to the muzzle with red hot facts waiting our command. If God shall give the friends of this cause intelligence and patience to lay the facts lovingly on the hearts of the American people, they will make a response that will drown forever the hissing innuendoes of the old serpent.

The argument for prohibition rests upon what is everywhere conceded the natural right of self-preservation. On this right, one of the chief pillars of the whole social fabric, we demand the removal of the constant menace to human life involved in the liquor traffic. It puts life in peril in two ways: First, by a direct assault upon it. By this traffic an article is exposed for sale which all chemists, as anyone may see by consulting authorities, class as a deadly poison. A vast number of animals have been sacrificed by scientific experiments to prove the true nature of alcohol, as though its terrible ravages in the human system were not enough to settle the question. The dog, the rabbit, and even the cat, with its nine lives, in countless numbers, have been made to pass through the fires of experiment in honor of king alcohol, and their departed shades send back a faithful warning to their old masters, many of whom, not satis-

fied with the results of the experiment with these irra-
tional animals, persist in trying it upon their own persons.   Poisons are known as such only by observing
their effects upon living organisms, and by this process,
alcohol is classed by scientists among the deadly poisons.
But this article, often in a highly diluted state, without
proper label or warning as to its true character, is
exposed to public sale as a beverage, under such conditions as to conceal its deadly qualities, and secure the
patronage of a large number of unsuspecting persons.
Its venders push their traffic with unflagging zeal and
specious arguments.   It is recommended to the young
as exhilarating and life giving ; to the feeble as a restorer
of lost vigor; to the weary as a support in excessive toil ;
to those subject to great exposure as a protection against
heat, cold, dampness, malaria and contagion ; to the slug-
gish as a great quickener of thought and feeling ; to
those about to encounter unusual demands upon their
strength as doubling human power for special emergen-
cies, and as an important aid in the ordinary experiences
of every day life ; as a protection against monotony,
ennui, and the invisible evils that lurk about every life.
So well do its first effects sustain these pretentions that
it does not fail to secure an enormous sale, and to conceal its true character till it has sent its fatal dart
through the confiding heart of its victim.   It is this false
pretense, this deception that makes the traffic responsible
for the destruction that follows, and that justifies the extreme measure of prohibition.   The miserable victims who
go down to a drunkard's grave ought to have known better, but these pretenses deceived them, and are deceiving
many of our brightest minds to-day.   You can never be
sure that Christian education, training and culture have

brought safety to your home, for this deception invades the highest places, even the pulpits of the sanctuary, casting down some of the most gifted men who have stood up to plead the cause of God with their fellow-men. There is only one way to secure that personal safety, to which all have a natural right, and that is to put away the destroyer. The second peril to life is from an indirect assault upon it. If, indeed, you are proof against the wiles of the charmer, your life is not thereby exempt from peril. He stands in your street night and day with a drawn sword in his hand, and may strike you down at any moment. Standing upon your door step, some maudlin creature issuing from the saloon may, with random pistol shot, lay you low. As you go to business the saloon row may burst into conflagration just as you pass the door, and you be its innocent victim. If you travel, a drunken engineer may swamp your boat or wreck your train. If you would drive into the park, a drunken driver may dash wildly into your vehicle or throw you over a precipice. There is no place you can go, or sit, or sleep, where your life is not in constant peril from this traffic. Men have been smitten down by it in all the secure places where they have consoled themselves upon their safety. Our argument is that we have a right to protection from this peril by banishing the cause of it from society. We accept the perils of large manufactories, of massing heavy populations in large cities, of railway travel, because they are necessary to human welfare, and because it has been proven by experience that they confer great benefits upon society far out-weighing all incidental evils. But of the liquor traffic no man has any good to allege in extenuation of its peril to human life. It is the great corruptor of morals, the disturber of social order, the foe of domestic happiness, a blight upon material prosperity, and the destroyer of life. I ask, then, upon what ground am I expected to put my life in peril by tolerating it in my street? What service is it rendering to humanity to justify this sacrifice on my part? I make a solemn complaint to my fellow citizens, in my own and in behalf of the race, that this destroyer is abroad in the land, and ask for their suffrages in favor of banishing him. If we refuse and allow the work of destruction to go on, we are partakers in the guilt of every murder committed. It is estimated that one hundred thousand people come to their death every year in this country from the effects of strong drink. This is a larger number than fell in battle any one year of the recent Civil War. And oh! what a death! "Not for country, home and sacred honor!" Every one of the hundred thousand dies dishonored, leaving a heritage of shame to their posterity, and the influence of their lives to all the worst elements of society. We do not realize it because it is not with beating drums, flying banners, marching armies, and thundering artillery, but quietly, singly,—in the alleys, garrets, after they have made themselves objects of loathing of which society is glad to be rid, that these poor wretches by the hundred thousand annually go to graves that know no annual decoration day, with long processions, stirring music and elaborate eulogies. How earnestly we prayed for the war to cease! How wicked seemed the destruction of so many lives! It lasted but four years, but for twenty-five we have been talking of its enormities, and protesting to Heaven against its cruelties and wrongs, yet through all these twenty-five years this more terrible destruction has been going on by our consent. It is in our own streets, and we have known of it, and consented to it. Is there any greater wonder among men, any more monstrous and wicked absurdity, than that the free American people, casting every year a ballot that is as the voice of God in determining what shall be tolerated under our government, have allowed this work of destruction to continue? If now the country will pause to think about this, and not meet it as the criminal does when brought face to face with his crime, with a sneer, with the cry of "fanaticism! fanaticism!" "absurd!" if we will think about it long enough to get at the truth, and to feel its force, there is virtue enough in the American people to rise to the demands of the occasion. The argument is unanswerable. There are no grounds on which to justify the continued toleration in society of a traffic that is in open war with human life. But if we broaden the range of our vision and consider the interests of society at large, the argument is not less conclusive. The right of self-preservation belongs to society as well as to individuals. This is the axiomatic principle upon which, as a cornerstone, the whole structure of civil society rests. It not only has the right, but it is bound by every consideration to the duty of enacting such laws as are necessary for its preservation and peace. Society in its organized capacity has a quarrel with the saloon that can never be satisfactorily settled but by its expulsion. There is great unrest, apprehension, conflict and suffering wherever the saloon exists, and society writhes and groans with pain till it is cast out. It not only inflicts innumerable evils upon society, but it also imposes great burdens in consequence of them which it ought not to bear.

Idiocy and insanity are greatly increased where the

saloon holds sway, and the community must bear a cor-responding heavy tax to support these unfortunate vic-tims of intemperance. Intelligence quits its home in the .brain of man, and reason indignantly resigns its throne, where such a foe to every human interest is given cordial recognition, and the idiotic stare and the meaningless mumble of incoherent sounds declare that humanity will abdicate rather than capitulate to such a barbaric foe. How merciful is nature to deny in some cases to the child of the drinker the possession of the faculties which would make possible the inheritance of the appetite which in his father destroyed every noble quality and developed every base passion. Of three hun-dred idiots in the state of Massachusetts Dr. Howe referred one hundred and forty-five directly to intemper-ance, and a like proportion of the insane was referred to the same cause. The number of idiots in the United States is seventy-six thousand eight hundred and ninety-five, and we may suppose that a like per cent. of this number is due to the effects of the deadly poison which science teaches makes a direct attack upon the brain, and works against all the noblest and with all the basest elements in human nature. Society has not only the right, but it is solemnly bound to free itself from this evil, which strikes at its intellectual soundness and its financial resources as well in the same blow.

In every age pauperism has been one of the great evils and burdens of civilized society. In every county and city of this broad land the traveller will see large buildings and ample grounds provided and maintained by the public for the care of this class. Some are brought into this class through intellectual or physical imbecility, others by loss of property, others by bereavement, others by loss of self-respect and will power through intemperance or other indulgence. The student of pauperism will find that it has a strong affinity for the saloon. There are in the United States sixty-seven thousand and sixty-seven paupers, a vast and hideous army, and enormous sums are required for their support. It is a fair estimate to credit three-fourths of all this number of paupers and of this outlay of money to the use of intoxicating drinks. No unprejudiced mind can properly consider this case without coming to the conclusion that society ought to banish this source of pauperism, and protect itself from further demoralization and loss from that which gives nothing back in compensation for the evil it does.

The greatest evil from which society suppers is the crime that works like a poison in its veins, and eats like a cancer at its vitals. Criminal arrests, prosecutions, incarcerations and executions are every day events. Courts, jails and penitentiaries are prominent and costly institutions of society. Policemen, sheriffs, constables, attorneys and judges everywhere abound. A ceaseless war is carried on against all that makes for virtue, order, peace and prosperity, and the terrible cost of maintaining this war is laid upon the society against which it is waged. Those who have known most of this dark subject of human crime, who have had the best opportunities for looking behind the scenes, have been most pronounced in regard to the complicity of the saloon with all the worst elements at work in society. There comes but one testimony from the judges on the bench —those impartial students of crime, whose rare opportunities for learning its true origin and inspiration entitle them to speak with authority, and justify our fullest

confidence. In all the great centers of population in
England and in America, where drunkenness and crime
most abound, they agree in the statement that from
three-fourths to nine-tenths of all crimes committed are
due to the influence of strong drink. Anyone who fre-
quents the police courts, or the criminal courts of our
large cities, will not need the testimony of a judge to
instruct him upon this subject. Written on the very
faces and persons of the criminal classes he may read
the history of their alliance with strong drink. Many
of the worst criminals have testified that they shrank
from the deeds that filled society with horror, and never
could have committed them had they not been nerved
and stimulated to it by repeated draughts of strong
drink. They could not strike the fatal blow till the sensibilities were deadened and the passions inflamed by the
spirit of all evil. It is a known fact also that many
men who are very orderly and virtuous when sober,
become fiends incarnate when under the influence of
strong drink, and deeds are done of which they would
blush to think in their sober moments. Under the influence of intoxicants reason is dethroned, passion is stimulated, men become other than themselves, turn their
backs upon their whole history, reverse all the principles of their past lives, throw away the good name they
were a lifetime in winning, and strike down their most
cherished friends. These are the simple indisputable
facts of every day occurrence in communities where the
saloon exists, and they lay a foundation for the prohibition argument which no sophistry can move. The testimony of all communities where prohibition has had a
fair trial, is that it diminishes crime and elevates the
moral tone of society. From Maine, from Kansas, from

Iowa and from Atlanta comes the testimony that crimes against life and the peace of society cease, that jails are empty, and that officers of the law have little to do, while there is a corresponding decrease in the taxes that burden society. The argument is unanswerable, and it is one of the strangest mysteries of civilized society, how an intelligent, conscientious people with a free ballot in their hands, have consented so long to harbor such a corruptor of its morals and such a disturber of its peace as the saloon has proven to be. What strange infatuation has fallen upon society? Who can account for the apathy and indifference in good people that sit still while this monster marches through the streets corrupting and killing? How can anyone hold himself guiltless of the violence, theft, licentiousness and murder springing from this source, unless he has done all in his power to cast it out of society?

There yet remains the financial argument. Every question must come to this test, be weighed in the money changer's scales, and, answer the interrogation, "will it pay?" While it may not be the highest consideration, with many minds it is the most influential, and it has a legitimate place in every honest and thorough discussion. A high moral nature may still adhere tenaciously to the cause of truth though it clearly involves financial ruin, but even bad men must despise and reject a cause which is not only morally bad in every phase, but which also stands for the waste of substance and the overthrow of material prosperity. The liquor traffic is the ally of every vice, is a copartner with criminals of every class, is abhorrent to all high moral feeling, but in addition to this it is the greatest blight upon material prosperity known in civilized countries. The calculation of the loss it inflicts runs up

into amounts so vast that the mind fails to follow the
growing numbers, and is utterly unable to comprehend
their significance. The figures representing the waste
of the liquor traffic, like those employed to express
astronomical distances, are so vast as to produce no definite, intelligible impression on the mind. To say that
the sun is ninety-three millions of miles from the earth
conveys no definite knowledge, for no man can in his
mind measure off that many miles, form a mental picture
or conception of them, and thus really know what is
implied in the statement. The stars twinkle in depths
that mock our power of conceiving of numbers and distance. So when we come to compute the losses of the
liquor traffic, and the amount runs up into the millions,
we lose all power of forming a mental conception of the
numbers with which we are dealing. If we put aside all
moral, philanthropic and patriotic considerations, and
look at this question from the counting-room standpoint
we have such an argument as no financial secretary was
ever able to present to his political supporters. All
sentimentalism aside, and the cold facts of statistical tables
are overwhelming. The last United States census shows
that the sale of strong drink reached the enormous sum
of $900,000,000.

This calculation is based on the sale of liquors as
reported in bulk, but as all know in the retail sale they
are adulterated so that the actual cost to the people is
very much larger. Some have placed the estimate for
the yearly drink bill as high as $1,200,000,000, but it is
probably nearer the truth to give $900,000,000 as the
approximate sum. This sum is so vast that we can
have but little notion of it. This drink bill for two
years would pay the entire national debt and leave a

large surplus in the treasury. It may help our imaginations to form some conception of it to say that if this amount were spent in buying flour it would furnish five barrels to every man, woman and child, or an average of twenty-five barrels to every family in the land. If the barrels were placed end to end there would be enough to girdle the earth five times. Is it strange that with such an insane and wicked waste of the bounty of heaven, there should be poverty and want, and many people going up and down the land talking of an "anti-poverty party?" The real anti-poverty movement is found in the temperance cause. Convert your whiskey into bread, your beer into clothing, and there will be little poverty left. The average cost to the family of the drinking man, aside from loss by sickness, non-employment and other indirect causes is $250 per year. Is it strange if the judgments of heaven fall on the land, if there are riots, strikes, great distress and commotion, while this all-devouring conflagration rages in the homes of the people? What wonder if the whole land is yet wrapped in one sheet of flame if we thus allow the fires of hell to be kindled in our homes? But we have noticed only one feature of the annual drink bill, the direct expenditure. There are more than 500,000 men engaged in the liquor business, all agents for the propagation of the drinking habit, interested to make their business successful, if for nothing else. This great army of men, enough to found an empire, is taken from the productive industries of the country, and all their toil and business talent employed to impoverish, disease, corrupt and debase the people of the land. Estimating their wages at $1.50 per day, they entail an annual loss upon the country of $225,000,000. There is also another great army not so well organized and disciplined as this, nor so well clothed or fed, but equally devoted to the cause, though from other considerations.   A hideous body of camp followers, hangers on, with disfigured faces, defiled clothing, vile speech and abandoned habits, wrecked hopes and lost manhood, the product and sup-port of the saloon, the fruit and proof of the business, sweeping off in almost endless lines, or swaying about in eddying groups as a beer keg happens to establish a center of attraction; the great drunkard's army of 700,000, all with halters about their necks waiting their turn to swing and then drop into the ditch.   If we allow these men half their time for work at $1.50 per day, we have from them a loss of $157,500,000.   But do these armies fight no battles?   Do they commit no depredations upon the rich surrounding territory of the temperance loving public?   Every street and highway is lined with police-men, sheriffs, constables and officers of the law to protect society, and yet night is made hideous and the day full of peril, by outbreaks of violence and deeds of cruelty and shame.   Jails, penitentiaries and court proceedings, to take a low view of them, all cost money, and it is a low estimate to charge the crimes due to intemperance with an annual cost of $100,000,000.   Our counties and cities provide for a great multitude of drunken paupers, 800,000 men with all of manhood ripped out of them, till they are not even equal to the beasts and birds that pro-vide for themselves, and this costs the tax paying public at least $100,000,000.   Then there are the idiots, the insane, the sick in hospitals, and many other sources of waste not counted.   The aggregate thus calculated reaches the inconceivable sum of $14,825,000,000.   Let us not forget that this is the smallest feature in the cost of the traffic. Let us remember that every dollar of this vast sum covers a festering cancer eating into the heart of the people. The base of this pyramid of gold rests on ruined homes, broken hearts, and dishonored graves, while its summit is forever shrouded in a black cloud of sighs, groans, bitter curses and dying imprecations. The men who fall in battle are only the faintest index to the cruelty of war. The sad homes, the broken hearts and the mourning friends can never be numbered nor estimated. So here, great as is the cost, it seems trivial in comparison with the incalculable woe of which it is a faint index. But confining our thought to the matter of cost, let us compare it with the amounts paid for the necessaries of life, and see if we may thus help ourselves to a clearer conception of its magnitude. The value of all the live stock of the country, the horses, mules, cattle, sheep and hogs is just about the amount of this annual drink bill. The total wages of the laboring classes, the hard earned support of the families of the toiling masses, too much of which finds its way into the till of the saloon, amounts to less than four-fifths of the money spent for that which "satisfieth not." All the money spent for food and food products does not amount to one-half the amount given for that which would have been dear if obtained without cost. The people pay annually for clothing, only about one-fourth as much as they burn up on the altars of Bacchus. Considerably less is spent for boots, shoes, hosiery, hats, cotton and woolen goods, and for food than is thrown into this maëlstrom. In these overwhelming facts, set forth not in the fervid speech of temperance orators, but in the cold unsentimental census of the United States, the temperance argument has a foundation which no

assaults can move. The perversion of facts to which
the enemies of this cause continually resort, is here
apparent, in the fact that they constantly cry out against
temperance advocates as fanatics. These facts tower to
the heavens, yet the men who announce them and
endeavor to show their significance are branded as
fanatics! The Devil inviting the Son of God to fall
down and worship him is the only historic parallel to
the audacity of this insult to the truth. The only
wonder is that with such overwhelming arguments temperance advocates have not been more earnest, and have
not pushed their cause with more vigor. To the men
who think that the times are not pregnant with great
subjects, that opportunities for great achievements do
not now appear, who stand sighing for the return of such
circumstances as gave a field for the genius of Webster,
Sumner, Lincoln and Grant, we commend this cause.
There never was a better opportunity for genius, courage, philanthropy and for all the qualities that enter
into true greatness. Let me commend to our aspiring
politicians who are looking for a chance to serve the
people, for a great cause worthy of their powers, for an
opportunity to gain the noble ranks of the world's great
heroes, this great cause, even now at the door with
torn feet and dust covered garments, having come over
a long and difficult road, it stands waiting for some one
to plead its claims before the high court of the American
conscience. The man who shall stop the annual waste
of these millions of money will write his name high on
the roll of fame, and will stand in history as one of the
greatest benefactors of the nation.

CHAPTER V.

MORAL RIGHT.

IF prohibition involves the violation of the rights of those engaged in the liquor traffic, we should pause and consider the case well before giving our voice in its favor. It is an error in principle and in policy "to do evil that good may come." The worst men have rights, and the rights of the bad are sacred as those of the good. The fact that one is a liquor seller, does not release us from the obligation to do justly by him. Great as his evil doing may be, he has a right to the protection of the laws of the land until formally condemned to suffer their penalty. It is the function of government to protect the rights and the property of the citizen. It is cruel tyranny to pervert the office of government, and employ it for the oppression and robbery of the private citizen. It is claimed that the enactment of prohibition would interfere with the business interests of a large class, and render valuable properties worthless. This fact has been urged against it as a great injustice and wrong. In the discussion that prevailed prior to the vote in Ohio upon the proposed prohibition amendment to the constitution, this objection was urged with great force, as it was said that the adoption of the amendment would render $100,000,000 of property worthless. Those engaged in the manufacture and sale of strong drinks have raised a great outcry against the injustice of prohibition wherever it has been proposed. "What! do

you propose to rob us? Will you destroy our property,
beggar our wives and children, and leave us no means of
support? Will you not have a little mercy if unwilling
to give us justice?" Many excellent people are not a
little affected by this cry of distress, and without stopping carefully to consider its fallacy are ready to concede
the justice of the protest. Deep earnestness in an
appeal, especially if addressed to the sympathies, has to
many minds the practical force of profound argument.
Many good people start back and say, however desirable
the ends to be secured by prohibition, they cannot consent to a policy that would bring disaster and injustice
to their neighbors. Yes, the business these men have
been at for years is beginning to come home to them
and they are troubled; they have loved destruction and
it is at their own doors. The cycle of Divine justice is
just completing itself, and the injustice and wrong
inflicted upon women and children who cried to heaven
night and day for protection from the evils of the liquor
traffic, are coming home to their authors, demanding
settlement in the name of the King Eternal. The
claim is presented through the awakened conscience of
the people, with a vigor that indicates force back of it to
enforce it. Once pleading women and ragged children
stood begging these men to spare their homes, to allow
them bread and clothing, but they scorned these helpless
suppliants. They planted their traffic by the side of the
home, the school and the church, and drew into it by
the aid of their great deceiver, the substance of very
good and beautiful thing upon which they could lay their
hands. Whence came these great properties for which
protection is so loudly claimed in the name of justice?
They have been accumulated and built up by the very

process against which they now so loudly declaim, by the destruction and absorption of the property of others. Every stone, brick and board was wrenched out of the hand of the unfortunate victim of the appetite for strong drink, with no compensation but an increase of fuel for the flame that was consuming him. It was taken without giving a just equivalent, by deception and intoxication the victim was made willing and glad to part with everything he possessed, and these men were as glad to receive it. It is, therefore, the robber's booty, and it may be justly taken and destroyed.

Study these properties, read their histories. See what a blight fell on the properties of the surrounding community as their vast proportions took form and rose in magnificence before the public eye. There a respectable merchant began to share his profits in a secret way with the saloon. The infatuation grew till all the profits were taken, then this deadly cancer began to eat into the principal, health and the peace of home began to go, till at last the sheriff walked in and sold to the highest bidder what was left of the best stock of goods in the town. There the only son of an honest farmer, who has just inherited and moved into the old homestead, is enticed by the wily destroyer, who serpent-like said, as to Eve, "thou shalt not surely die." He began to loiter away his time and to spend his money at the village saloon, and the farm begins to show neglect. Those who knew the place when it was kept by the father who now lies in the church-yard, shake their heads as they pass by. Soon the horses and the cattle must be sold to pay the bill at the saloon. At last a mortgage is invited and refuses not to come as a copartner in the business, soon to become sole proprietor in the interests of the

4

saloon. There a laboring man, whose wages just maintain his large family, is induced by the example of the
merchant and the farmer, who sometimes employ him, to
loiter at the saloon and to take the maddening bowl to
his lips. His wages and his time are taken, then the
wages of his children, driven from school to hard work,
then the wages of his wife earned at the wash tub, all goes
into the coffers of these same disturbed property holders;
finally there comes a day when there is crape on the
door of a miserable hovel, and a drunkard's funeral is
conducted in a place from which everything of beauty
or value has been taken. Around these properties such
scenes constantly occur, and from them they derive their
very being.

Do you see that splendid mansion? The distiller
lives there. The foundation was contributed by the
manufacturer across the way, whose mill stands idle
while his executors are endeavoring to save something
from the estate for the heart-broken widow. The walls
were given by three once highly respected business men;
one lies in a drunkard's grave, one is in the penitentiary,
and the other is a street vagabond. Two farmers put
on the roof by selling out their farms, moving into garrets in the city, and sending out their daughters to service. The windows of French plate were put in by the
savings of six mechanics for ten years deposited at the
corner grocery, the depositors taking a receipt entitling
them to free admission to any of the poor houses or
insane asylums of the land. The floors were laid by the
daily offerings of ten laboring men, who hold a receipt in
full entitling them to a drunkard's grave and burial in
any cemetery at public expense. The carpets were
woven from the wedding dresses of fifty heart-broken,

disappointed wives, and from the clothing of an army
of ragged children who shiver through the street, their
only inheritance poverty, shame and a premature death.
The delicate coloring on the walls was captured from
the blooming cheeks of twenty happy brides, that having become marble, are now turning to dust. The fond
mothers of the town contributed their smiles, and the
little children the brightness of their eyes and faces to
furnish pictures for the walls suitable for such a place.
One minister, three lawyers and as many physicians
gave pulpit, briefs and pill bags to construct the tower.
This is the property in behalf of which the cry of
"justice" is raised. If God shall hear the cry and
grant it justice there will not be left one stone upon
another. While these walls were rising the cry for
justice, aye for mercy, came from many blighted homes,
but they were not regarded, and now that those who
would not hear the cry of distress are themselves the
suppliants, the even balances of eternal rectitude will
return them such measure as they meted out to others.
These bitter prayers which no man would hear wrung
from the hearts of helpless women and children poured
into the ears of men, then lifted to God, breathed out
into the night air, mingling with every tempest that
swept by, were living seeds from the very heart's sore
that were sure to find a lodging place somewhere in the
universe, where they would grow and bring forth fruit,
that when fully ripe would fall at the door of the men
by whom they were rejected. To those who "love
cursing," cursing shall be the portion of their cup.
These men delighted in wasting and absorbing the property of others by a shrewd device which they called
business, and when the cycle of eternal truth completes

itself, as soon it must, these accumulated properties will themselves by legal process be taken from those who hold them unjustly, and returned to society for other and lawful uses. "The revenges of history" and the natural apprehensions of the human mind, as well as the Word of God, which declares " with what measure ye mete, it shall be measured to you again," teach us to expect such a vindication of moral righteousness even in this world. There can be no doubt about the source from which this property was derived, neither can there be as to the intention of those by whom it was accumulated. If it could be shown that they did not understand the nature of the traffic in which they were engaged, that they did not know what desolation spread abroad wherever it existed, there might be an excuse for them. But they exposed for sale an article which they knew had no intrinsic value, which they also knew had great power over the weaknesses and vices of men, leading them to part with daily food, clothing, houses and lands, the inheritances of their ancestors, and to destroy their bodies and damn their souls that they might obtain it. It was their knowledge of this marvelous power of the article they exposed to sale, to command purchasers at any price that induced them to invest their capital in the business. The dry goods business fluctuates with the times and requires great skill to win success. An iron mill must stand still when depression comes or while the strike lasts, and may yield a fortune or bankruptcy. Even the farmer has his droughts, blights and empty garners. But here is a business that is proof against drouth, depression never reaches it, men never strike against it. hard times are unknown to it, business here goes on forever with little question about price or

quality of goods. The proprietors well understand that
their patrons are so devoted to them that nothing will
divert them, that they will rob the wardrobe and larder
of the home, and even send out wife and children to the
most menial service rather than diminish their purchases. It was a knowledge of this fact, that profits
were large and sure, that a comfortable living could be
easily made that induced these men to enter the business. The poverty, shame, ruin and damnation that
would come to many were all distinctly seen; they
deplored these, but they wanted the money. They
regretted that anyone should suffer, as the highwayman
and the burglar does, but they coveted the profits of the
business. While murder and destruction result everywhere from the traffic, I freely grant that, as a rule, the
venders of strong drink deplore the fact, but for the
profit there is in the business they still continue it, well
knowing and in spite of these consequences. Murder,
nor indeed any other act of human wickedness is rarely
committed where the guilty party does not stand pre-
cisely upon this footing, regretting the evil that results,
but bent upon securing the alluring advantage. All
men look at the profit to be gained, rather than at the
evil results. Judas, whose name is a synonym for all
meanness and wickedness, looked only at the thirty
pieces of silver. He wanted them, resolved to have
them and succeeded in getting them. He wished no
harm to Christ, was deeply pained when he saw that
evil had come to him through his covetousness; with a
far nobler spirit and unlike many to whom clear evidence is brought that they have been trafficking in human
blood, he carried back the money to those from whom
he received it, and gave evidence of the genuineness of

his penitence by taking his own life. He meant no evil
to the Son of God, he wanted the thirty pieces of silver.
Do not the liquor dealers understand the case? Certainly they do. Never shall I forget the thrill of horror
that ran through my boyish frame as I heard an old
retired saloon keeper, in a swaggering, bantering way,
as indicating the success with which he had pushed his
business, declare that he knew twenty-four men who
died from drinking at his saloon. Recently a wholesale
dealer, one of the best of the class, in the city of Philadelphia, came home in the evening and engaged in con-
versation with a sewing woman in the house. She com-
plained of the hard times. "Yes," he said, "the times
are hard, but I have sold a hundred barrels of whiskey
to-day, all the same." Then laughing, said: "Oh!
wouldn't it be fun to see all the fights there are in that
hundred barrels of whiskey?" He saw and knew just
what kind of business he was doing. Talk with one of
these men honestly and sincerely and he will tell you as
they often have me, that it is the meanest business on
earth, that they only went into it to make money, and
that as soon as they make enough to enable them to do
so they will retire from it. The character and consequences of the business are clearly seen, but they brave
these for the money it yields. They know the facts
perfectly, the very heavens are red above the fires of
this conflagration, the earth is filled with the cry of the
distress it has produced, in every street the crape on the
door proclaims its work, smoldering ruins send up their
fumes as an announcement that the destroyer is abroad,
across every order for goods and on their own bill heads
the character of the business was stamped in indelible
characters. They have seen clearly that the wages of

the laboring man slipped through his hand into their pocket, that the will of the father conveying valuable property to the son was in fact but a bill of shipment for goods sure to be delivered to them in due time, that the heroines of the age, the wives and mothers of drunkards were in their superhuman efforts to support, cover the shame and possibly restore those dear to them, toiling for their profit, that they were stealing the color from the young wife's cheek, the joy from her heart and the hope from her sky—they saw it all, they intended it all, and as they loved cursing, cursing must be the portion of their cup.

The Devil has never perpetrated so grim a joke upon poor hoodwinked humanity as this cry for justice in behalf of the saloon. In God's name let every man join in the prayer, and stand back while the answer falls from heaven in the awakened conscience of the American people.

But they say "this is our business, our only means of making a living, it would be robbery to take our property from us without compensation." If a company of train robbers were overtaken in their hiding-place they might raise the same cry. "These weapons are the tools of our trade by which we make a living, and this treasure we have gained in the prosecution of our business, would you deprive us of the means of making a living? Will you not remember that wives and children are dependent upon us?" The one, of course, has a legal footing and the other has not, on this account the train robber is at a disadvantage with the saloon keeper, but on the principle of equity and before the enlightened conscience they stand on the same footing, unless, indeed, the advantage is in favor of the train robber. Consider how amiable a creature the train robber is. He walks into your car and presents a revolver at your head while you present him with your purse and watch, he gives you a moment to look into the gleaming steel muzzle and reflect on the brevity of human life, then passes on, making you unspeakably thankful for the mercy of God in sparing your life. The young man goes home to his mother without a stain upon his good name and with a thrilling experience to relate, a few months toil repairs the loss of his purse, and the next Christmas tree bears him a better watch than the one he lost. Infinitely worse is the fate of the young man who falls into the power of the saloon keeper. He is dishonored, covered with shame, his money taken, he is driven from business, is diseased, he becomes an object of terror or loathing in the home, and dies amid unspeakable horrors.

No one has ever disputed the moral right of seizing the tools and booty of train robbers, burglars and pirates, neither can any thoughtful man raise a question as to the moral right of destroying the liquor traffic. This traffic has existed and has been maintained for the purpose of destroying the property of others, and by the judgment and practice of all civilized nations it may justly be taken and destroyed. It is everywhere conceded as a principle of moral right, as in the case of burglars and pirates, that tools employed for preying upon the public and money accumulated in that way, may be seized by the public at will.

CHAPTER VI.

LEGAL RIGHT.

THE legal right of prohibition has been boldly contested on every field where it has been tried, and
though often re-affirmed by the highest legal authority,
it is still disputed. It would be amusing, if not a matter of such gravity, to see the friends of the deadly
traffic lift up their hands in holy horror against the
injustice and wrong of prohibition, and plead with their
fellow citizens in the name of law, equity and moral
right to resist it. Liquor sellers pleading for justice
and right match Satan quoting Scripture to the Son of
God, and is equally intended as a shrewd scheme of
deception. There is in it at least this tribute to the
friends of temperance, an open confession on the part of
our enemies that no argument will have influence with
us that is not based on these high moral grounds; and
there is in it also this confession of weakness, that their
own weapons are no longer sufficient, and that a last
resort must be made to the armory of heaven. When
Satan becomes a preacher of righteousness, it is because
he sees some great defeat near at hand. When Calvary
and redemption rose above the horizon, he went to the
Son of God with his mouth full of Scripture and boldly
attempted to betray him, but from that day his kingdom
has been breaking to pieces. That men who have trampled upon every law concerning their business, the Sunday closing law, the law against selling to minors and

to the intoxicated, should turn about and so vehemently demand the protection of the law, is a confession both of the wickedness and meanness of the business. Every possible device has been resorted to for the purpose either of setting aside or of boldly trampling upon the law wherever prohibition has been adopted. If any technical defect could be found in the form of the enactment, or in the process of its adoption, it was pressed to the utmost. Suits were instituted and the "law's delay" employed in the hope of wearing out the patience of the friends of temperance. In every way it has shown itself the enemy of law and order. If the friends of prohibition have urged their cause, it has responded by advocating a license law instead, with certain restrictions requiring Sabbath closing, and other matters supposed to be for the peace of the community. But no sooner has it obtained the law which it dictated than it proceeds to violate its provisions. It shows its defiance and contempt of law, its utter failure to recognize its sacred and lofty character, by boldly employing money to corrupt legislatures and courts to enact and interpret laws in its interests. It employs its great wealth and mighty influence to prostitute the law-making power, failing in this it employs them to corrupt the courts, if unsuccessful here it boldly defies and tramples upon the law.

There is no greater solecism in civil government than a law which at the same time punishes murder, and protects the saloon out of which murders arise. Law exists for the purpose of preventing crime and wrong, and for the purpose of protecting and supporting virtue and right. To yoke such an angel of light to this Devil's car, the liquor traffic, is to insult every moral sense and to present the most absurd travesty upon the true idea of government to be found on any page of history. To exalt that which wars against all laws for the overthrow of the peace and order of society into a creature of the law, to be protected and defended by it, is to proceed by intelligent method to plant cancers in every human system in the interests of good health. The liquor traffic is in itself the great law breaker, and it is the most active and influential agent in society for the disregard of all law. The criminal classes find in it their great stimulus and support in their deeds of violence and wrong, while our court and prison records show it to be the source of most of the crimes from which society suffers. Dr. Hargraves, in his great book, "Our Wasted Resources," gives valuable statistics upon this point, some of which are here re-produced. They do not come down to date, and are from certain localities only, but they give a fair and truthful view of the general facts, and will apply to the principle under consideration for all localities and times.

"In an article prepared by A. S. Fisk, A. M., entitled, " The Relations of Education to Crime in New England, and the Facilities for Education in her Penal Institutions," and published in the report of the United States Commissioner of Education for the year 1871, page 549, we find the following:

"The fourth fact is that from 80 to 90 per cent. of our criminals connect their courses of crime with intemperance. Of the 14,315 inmates of the Massachusetts prisons, 12,396 are reported to have been intemperate, or 84 per cent."

"At the Deer Island House of Industry (Boston), not included in the above figures, of 3,514 committals, 3,097, or 88 per cent., were for drunkenness; fifty-four more as idle and disorderly, which commonly means under the influence of drink; seventy-seven for assault and battery, which means the same thing; and forty-eight as common night-walkers, every one of whom is also a common drinker. We have, therefore, of this prison a full 93 per cent. whose confinement is connected with the use of drink; and this may be taken as a not exaggerated sample of many municipal prisons. In the New Hampshire State Prison, sixty-five out of ninety-one admit themselves to have been intemperate. Reports were asked from every state, county, and municipal prison in Connecticut in the spring of 1871 in reference to the statistics of drinking habits among the inmates, and it was found that more than 90 per cent. had been in habits of drink by their own admission.

The warden of the Rhode Island State Prison, and county jailer, estimates 90 per cent. of the residents of his cells as drinkers.

From Vermont and Maine no reports have been secured; but they would not, if their prisoners were all interrogated, bring the estimate below 80 per cent.

It will still be remembered that these figures do not cover the mere temporary arrests for drunkenness, disorder, etc., nor the facts of the municipal place of detention, where the percentage of drunken criminals will be most striking.

There is no enormity or crime to which persons, no matter how well disposed and gentle at other times, may not be impelled when under the influence of drink.

Husbands and fathers are not only caused to neglect wives and families, but to inflict upon them the most revolting cruelties. The affections in families are blunted and obliterated; children are neglected and left without clothing, food, or education, and often forced into crime by their parents to procure money for them to spend in drink; or they are abandoned and left to shift for themselves, and under the guidance of wicked associates are urged to commit crime to eke out a shiftless existence.

There can be no doubt in the minds of any who have examined the subject in the least but that the liquor traffic is the main source and prolific cause of the criminality that is steadily increasing from year to year, and which consequently necessitates the increase and enlargement of prisons and police officers. All of which has again and again been fully and clearly established by the testimony of judges, grand juries, police magistrates, chaplains, governors, and inspectors of prisons. They have repeatedly testified that frauds, embezzlements, theft, the prostitution of our young women, robberies, burglaries, and murders, are produced mainly by the brutalizing and depraving influences of strong drinks. More than three-fourths of the inmates of prisons attribute their fall to the use of intoxicating drinks. Of the 39 cases of murder and 121 cases of assault to murder in the city of Philadelphia in 1868, in almost every case it may be safely said that the murderer was intoxicated when the deed was committed. These bloody deeds were clearly traceable to the liquid poison that maddens the brain, depriving of reason, and leading to the commission of acts of blood and violence, at the thoughts of which, when sober and clothed in their right minds, the perpetrators' souls would revolt. They would say with one of old, "Is thy servant a dog that he should do this great thing?" For all these evils flowing from the liquor traffic not only do heavy and fearful responsibilities rest upon the liquor sellers, who entice, by various means, men and women to enter their places and indulge in strong drink ; but a terrible responsibility is also laid at the door of the law makers, citizen voters, and everyone who does not exert all his influence, political, social, and religious, against legalizing such traffic.

Reader, do you doubt that intoxicating drink produces the crimes charged against it ? If you do, examine well the following figures and facts.

The Brewers' Congress and the Liquor Dealers' Associations boast of the great revenue they pay for the privilege of selling liquors. The amount paid for tavern licenses in Pennsylvania in 1867 was $279,532 ; for beer licenses, $40,482—making a total of $320,015. Of this sum $162,746 was paid in Philadelphia. During that year, of 36,333 persons arrested in the city of Philadelphia, 13,930 were committed to prison for drunkenness who were not able to pay their fines, etc., but were incarcerated at the expense of the public. There were committed to the Philadelphia County Prison, from the 1st January, 1868, to January 1, 1869, for drunkenness, vagrancy, disorderly conduct, and breaches of the peace, 9,220. In the year 1867, as already seen, Pennsylvania paid for criminal and pauper expenses caused directly by liquor-drinking, $2,259,910, or an average of $5.80 for each voter in the State. The same year Philadelphia paupers and criminals cost $1,500,000, or $11 for each voter. What did Philadelphia receive in the way of revenue from license towards paying this million and a half of dollars? Nothing. The money paid for licenses went into the State treasury. The State received $317,742.75 for licenses to sell liquor, and paid for pauperism and crime caused by the use of strong drinks,

$2,259,910 ; or, in other words, the State from licenses received 14 cents, and spent one dollar for crime and pauperism. Truly, the State paid dear for its whistle. But, to be more specific in our charges against the liquor trade, we will present a few facts from official records.

The report of the Board of State Charities of Pennsylvania for 1871, on page 89, says: "The most prolific source of disease, poverty and crime, observing men will acknowledge, is intemperance. In our hospitals, as well as in our almshouses and prisons, a large portion of the inmates have reached the refuge in which they are found by the way of habitual intoxication." . . . "Intemperance, the great scourge of society, is, as every one knows, a social vice. Few inebriates begin their downward career by purchasing the stimulant in quantity, and taking it home to use at pleasure or convenience. The habit of its use is contracted in some public place where like companions meet, and where the exhilaration which strong drink produces may expand itself into boisterous mirth."

"The policy of giving licenses to certain parties to open taverns, where intoxicating drinks may be partaken of, and gatherings may be accommodated for their indulgence, is now in vogue." "The imposts exacted for these licenses are a source of considerable revenue." . . . . On page 90 the report says: "It would be difficult to name any practical good which results from this system (of licensing liquor-shops), unless it be that it furnishes a certain amount of revenue. Should these wages of iniquity be put into the treasury? They are the price of blood, and, in their aggregate, would be inadequate to buy fields enough to bury the multitudes who are the victims of the dreadful traffic for whose profits they sell the people's sanction." "And what economist can fail to discern, without any elaborate calculation, that the State is impoverished by the whole transaction? There is received into the public coffers a small tribute from every man who cares to secure the common authority for the prosecution of this pernicious trade, and the consequence is that there is lost from the commonwealth the productive labor of thousands who waste, in the licensed haunts of intemperance, both the ability to add to her wealth and the accumulations of former thrift."

Everywhere the testimony is that nine-tenths of all cases of vagrancy, disorderly conduct, and breaches of the peace, are the direct effects of intoxicating drinks; hence, 3,042 of the 3,380 cases of these offences were due to drink. These, added to the cases of intoxication, will give a total of 6,726 cases, or 88 per cent., as the direct results of the liquor traffic.

These startling facts deserve and demand the consideration of every one in the community, and should particularly impress our legislators with the necessity of adopting such measures as will tend to change this sad and terrible state of affairs, if not for the sake of humanity, at least for the financial interests of the country. If it costs so much to support our helpless, poor and criminal population, the State should take the means to prevent and correct these evils.

The Philadelphia County Prison Report for 1871 says, page 16: "About the usual proportion of commitments for the past year may be placed to the account, either directly or indirectly, of intemperance. There were for *intoxication* 3,684, against 3,983 for 1870, 3,546 for 1869, and 2,025 for 1868; for vagrancy, 1,059, against

1,377 for 1870, 1,248 for 1869, and 1,093 for 1868 ; for assault and battery, 1,821, against 1,876 for 1870, 1,687 for 1869, and 1,462 for 1868; for disorderly conduct and breach of the peace, 2,321, against 5,398 for 1870, 7,360 for 1869, and 8,132 for 1868; for assault with intent to kill, 153, against 132 for 1870, 146 for 1869, and 121 for 1868. Of the entire number of commitments (13,171), nearly three-fourths, or 9,038, are traceable to intemperance; drunkenness being, with exceptions, a cause of the offences in the foregoing list. The aggregate of these offenses is considerably smaller than for the two preceding years, it having been in 1870, 12,266, and in 1869, 13,987 The falling off is chiefly in commitments for breach of the peace—a form of commitment which has to some extent been abandoned by COMMITTING MAGISTRATES under instructions from the Court of Quarter Sessions. It would be unfair to assume that the offences alluded to are exclusively attributable to intemperance; for crime and vagrancy and prisons are found in countries where drunkenness is comparatively rare. But it cannot be doubted that the unrestrained multiplication of temptations to crime in the unbridled sale of alcoholic drinks in our city is a fearful evil."

Mr. William J. Mullen, the well-known and highly-esteemed prison agent, in his report for 1870, says : " An evidence of the bad effects of this unholy business, may be seen in the fact that there have been *thirty-four* murders within the last year in our city alone, each one of which was *traceable to intemperance;* and one hundred and twenty-one assaults to murder proceeding from the same cause. Of over 38,000 *arrests* in our city within the year, *seventy-five per cent.* of this number were *caused by intemperance,* Of the 18,305 persons committed to

5

our prison within the year, more than two-thirds were the consequence of intemperance. Of this number, 2,517 *were for intoxication*. The whole number committed to our prison for the offence of drunkenness for the last twenty years was 184,966 persons.

"The whole amount of blood money which has been paid to our STATE TREASURER for the year 1869 for license to sell intoxicating liquors in this State was $329,211.77, of which over $200,000 was paid by our city for the privilege of contributing nearly a million and a half of dollars for the support of our criminals and pauper population, who are made such by the *use of intoxicating liquors*. If we add to this a fair proportion of the expenses of our charitable as well as criminal institutions of Philadelphia (a large proportion of which is in consequence of intemperance), we have an expenditure of over $2,500,000." Again Mr. Mullen says: "Ignorance and drunkenness are the real causes of nearly all the misery in the world. The last is immeasurably worse than all others combined; for such is the benumbing, stultifying, and crazing effect of inebriating drinks that they change a man of reason and feeling into a brutalized monster. Hence it is that the 'knife, the dagger, the bludgeon, and the pistol are in such frequent use; and in the domestic circle cruelty to children, wife-beating; and in many families at home horrors of every kind.' This is lamentably too true, as is proved by the cases that consume the time of our CRIMINAL COURTS, and is seen by the condition of society at large. No sooner have our courts disposed of one case of murder or assassination than the liquor shops furnish others to supply its place."

Judge Allison, in a speech delivered at a public meet-

ing in Philadelphia, November, 1872, speaking of the
evils of intemperance, and the duty of good citizens to
join in the efforts made to do away with the evils of
rum-selling and rum-drinking, said: "Intemperance is
upon our right hand and left; on the streets, north,
south, east and west, we see the lures to destruction, and
see that in this city to-night men are being hurried to
the drunkard's grave and the drunkard's doom. Shall
we be held guiltless if we do not stretch forth our hands
and use the means we possess to save our perishing fellow-men? There is a day coming when this question
cannot be evaded, but must be answered before an
impartial Judge. The lives of these poor drunkards
will then be in some measure chargeable to us. There
are few people who see the practical evil as we see it in
the criminal courts of this city. There we can trace
four-fifths of the crimes that are committed to the influence of rum. There is not one case in twenty where a
man is tried for his life in which rum is not the direct
or indirect cause of the murder. *Rum* and *blood*—I
mean the shedding of blood—go hand in hand.

"Shall we not attempt to remedy this thing? Or
shall we close our eyes while the agencies for the sale of
rum are multiplied? Rum is already a mighty power
in this city, and it requires all the power of temperance men to put the traffic under bonds."

The Grand Jury for the December term, 1874, of the
Court of Quarter Sessions of the City of Philadelphia,
in the final presentment, said they "had acted upon 471
bills, of which 324 have been returned as true bills, and
147 have been ignored.

"A large proportion of the cases before us were for
assault and battery, and in every instance these were the

direct results of a free and improper use of intoxicating drinks. Indeed, this liquor traffic is the fertilizing source of all crime. It is evident that in a community where a considerable proportion of the people are unable from various causes to resist the temptation which beguiles them at every corner, there should be proper safeguards as a defence for the weak ones. In the protection of society from the devastations of this river of fire, it may yet be necessary to hold the liquor seller to a criminal responsibility for the crimes committed under the influence of liquors sold by him or them.

"Society must be protected, purified and elevated from present conditions by wise, intelligent and far-reaching agencies, religious, social and legislative. It is a noticeable fact that a very considerable number of these crimes were committed on the Sabbath day; so that the historic consequences which in all ages have followed Sabbath desecration are ripening their poison-fruit in our midst. Statistics well kept constantly show that no legislation of city or state, no social or human contrivance, can for a moment arrest the certain punishment which marches like an armed giant in the path of an ever-present Divine retribution. The Sabbath of God cannot be desecrated with impunity by either individuals, corporations, or governments.

"A growing evil and fruitful source of crime in our city arises from the thousands of idle, vagrant youth who wander about the city and congregate in dens of infamy. These are the products, for the most part, of broken and disrupted families, shattered and consumed by the liquid fires of rum. This is a dangerous element in our midst, young, vigorous, and, to some extent, equipped. The well-being of our city imperatively demands the instant suppression of the dens where these youths are harbored, and the lowest instincts ministered to and trained to crime. It is clear that when, from crime or other causes, the parent ceases to control or to provide for, educate, and properly train the child, then the state or city government becomes of right and duty the parent, and is bound to enter fully into all the responsibilities and relationship of parent to child. What, then, shall be said of the city parent, rich in palace homes, and overflowing with wealth and prosperity, yet with 15,000 of her youth beggars, thieves, homeless? The only remedy at our hand is COMPULSORY EDUCATION; not a house of correction, but a school. Ignorance is very expensive; crime still more so. Juvenile crime is the most expensive. In a mere dollar sense it would cost much less to the taxpayer to arrest, confine and educate into societary salvation these children of the street and den than it now does under the present conditions. These wretched outcasts are the city's children."

This is a question about law, and a lawyer's opinion concerning it is of value. Our "friends the enemy" have done us good service at this point. By carrying their case into the supreme judicatures they have called forth decisions from the highest authorities, that settle forever the question of constitutionality and legal right.

The following extracts are from the records of the Supreme Court of the United States:

Chief-Justice Taney said:

"If any State deems the retail and internal traffic in ardent spirits injurious to its citizens, and calculated to produce idleness, vice, or debauchery, I see nothing in the Constitution of the United States to prevent it from regulating or restraining the traffic, or from prohibiting it altogether, if it thinks proper."—5 *Howard*, 577.

Justice McLean said:

" A license to sell an article, foreign or domestic, as a merchant, or inn keeper, or victualler, is a matter of police and revenue, *within the power of the State.*"—5 *Howard*, 589. And again: "It is the settled construction of every regulation of commerce that, under the sanction of its general laws, no person can introduce into a community malignant diseases, or anything which contaminates its morals or endangers its safety."—*Ibid.* "If the foreign articles be injurious to the health or morals of the community, a State may in the exercise of that great and comprehensive police power which lies at the foundation of its prosperity, *prohibit the sale of it.*—*Ibid.* 592. "No one can claim a license to retail spirits as a matter of right."—*Ibid.* 597.

Justice Daniels said of imports that are cleared of all control of the government which permits their introduction: .

"They are like all other property of the citizen, and should be equally the subjects of domestic regulation and taxation, whether owned by an importer or his vender, or may have been purchased by cargo, package, bale, piece, or yard, or by hogsheads, casks, or bottles."—5 *Howard*, 614. In answering the argument that the importer purchases the right to sell when he pays duties to the Government, Justice Daniels continues to say: " No such right as the one supposed is purchased by the importer, and no injury in any accurate sense is inflicted on him by denying to him the power demanded. He has not purchased and cannot purchase, from the Government that which it could not ensure to him—a

sale independently of the laws and policy of the States."—
Ibid. 616.

Justice Woodbury said:

" After articles have come within the territorial limits
of States, whether on land or water, the destruction
itself of what constitutes disease and death, and the
longer continuance of such articles within their limits,
or the terms and conditions of their continuance, when
conflicting with their legitimate police, or with their
power over internal commerce or with their right of
taxation over all persons and property within their
jurisdiction, seems one of the first principles of State
sovereignty, and indispensable to public safety."—5
Howard, 630.

Justice Grier said:

" It is not necessary to array the appalling statistics
of misery, pauperism, and crime, which have their
origin in the use and abuse of ardent spirits. The police
power, which is exclusively in the State, is competent to
the correction of these great evils, and all measures
of restraint or prohibition necessary to effect that purpose are within the scope of that authority; and if a
loss of revenue should accrue to the United States from
a diminished consumption of ardent spirits, she will be
a gainer of a thousand-fold in the health, wealth, and
happiness of the people."—*Ibid.* 532.

While alchoholic stimulants are recognized as property,
and entitled to the protection of law, ownership in
them is subject to such restraints as are demanded by
the highest considerations of public expediency. Such
enactments are regarded as police regulations, established
for the prevention of pauperism and crime, for the
abatement of nuisances, and the promotion of public

health and safety. They are a just restraint of an injurious use of property which the legislature has authority to impose, and the extent to which such interference may be carried must rest exclusively in legislative wisdom where it is not controlled by fundamental law. It is a settled principle, essential to the rights of self-preservation in every organized community, that, however absolute may be the owner's title to his property, he holds it under the implied condition " that its use shall not work injury to the equal enjoyment and safety of others who have an equal right to the enjoyment of their property, nor be injurious to the community."—*Supreme Court New Jersey*, 1872.

"*Possessed of the power of absolute prohibition under the Constitution*, it seems to follow that any relaxation from a plenary exercise of such power, or qualified or conditional enactment by the legislature, by which license to sell may be obtained in the way and subject to the liabilities imposed by the act, cannot be an encroachment of legislative authority, unless, indeed, the legislature should transcend some settled principles of fundamental law respecting the trial or mode of prosecution or punishment of the party charged with an infraction of the provisions of the act, or with having incurred some liability under it. Acting in obedience to those fundamental principles, in accordance with which the guilt or liability of the party charged must first be ascertained and established, and the judgment of the law rendered against him, it seems competent for the legislature to attach such consequences, civil or criminal, to the mere act of sale as it pleases, even when such sale is made in pursuance of an authority of the legislature qualified or given for that purpose. *Empowered to pro-*

hibit entirely, the legislature may license *sub modo*, or conditionally only."— *Wisconsin Supreme Court*, 1873.

"Under what is called the police power, the leg sla-ture has the right to authorize the abatement of a pub-lic nuisance ; and the carrying on of an illegal traffic in intoxicating liquors, and the assembling of idle and vicious persons for that purpose is a nuisance, and may be so declared and abated according to law.—*Illinois Supreme Court*, 1873.

"In the exercise of its police power, a State has full power to prohibit, under penalties, the exercise of any trade or employment which is found to be hazardous or injurious to its citizens and destructive to the best interests of society, without providing compensation to those upon whom the prohibition rests."—*Michigan Supreme Court, The People vs. Hawley.*

It is a conceded principle in government, that society has the right to adopt such measures as are necessary to secure its highest good. On this principle it does enact prohibition against such buildings, such lines of business, such articles of commerce and such amuse-ments as are found to be dangerous to its interests. On this principle, so secure in the logic and history of the case, we rest our legal right to prohibit the liquor traffic.

The United States Supreme Court rendered a decision, Dec. 5, 1887, in three cases brought to it from Kansas, in which it reaffirms the right of a State to enforce prohibi-tion, even if it should entail heavy financial loss upon the manufacturer or dealer. This decision, in which the Court was practically unanimous, ought forever to settle the question of legal right.

CHAPTER VII.

INDIVIDUAL RIGHTS.

PERSONAL liberty is a sweet phrase that has been prostituted to base uses. To "be free indeed," in the enjoyment and practice of all human rights and duties, to live according to the highest ideals from inward impulse and inclination is the highest human attainment, but to apply this phrase to a course of life that binds every faculty, dethrones the will, debases the moral nature, and drags a man down against his most vigorous efforts to save himself from it, is a perversion of language and truth so monstrous that it can have originated only with the father of lies. There are, indeed, individual rights as distinct from the rights of society, rights with which society may not justly interfere. Society has a perfect right to regulate the conduct of the individual by law in so far as that conduct may affect the interests of others. There are many acts good in themselves, which society has no right to enjoin because they concern the individual alone, and do not affect society, save as it may be indirectly affected by the character of the individual of which they are an expression. There are also other acts distinctly wrong and wicked with which society may not interfere since they do not affect society. There is a realm of life beyond the supervision of society, where men are to be governed by the law of God and the teachings of their own consciences. A man's religious beliefs or forms of worship, so long as they do not interfere with social order, are above the supervision of society. If, as in the case of the Mormons, religious faith involves practices at war with the interests of society, it claims the right of excluding the objectionable feature. What passes in a man's own life of a purely subjective character, his thoughts, plans, purposes, passions and ambitions, society takes no thought of until they take objective form by an impact upon a fellow being, then society must act. Such a thing as absolute personal liberty does not exist, save in the imagination of those who rebel against law. The universe is a government, there is not. a grain of sand that is not under law and that does not obey it. God has given men a law for every impulse, thought and act. Then he gave to society authority to make laws for its own welfare. Thus, every man is held by the double bond of allegiance to God and to his race. If men were living solitary, things would be right to them which in society are wrong : for instance, they might dispense with clothing in a solitary state, but in society this would be wrong because offensive to the feelings and injurious to the morals of others. If a man chooses to go to some lone island of the sea and drink till he dies as a beast, society will leave him to the righteous judgment of Almighty God; it claims no supervision of a case of that kind. But when a man claims that privilege in society, and in its exercise puts himself in a state to injure life and property about him, society has an indefeasible right to come forward with an absolute prohibition. Society exists by its members agreeing to unite for the common welfare, to support what is for the common good, and to suppress what is inimical to it. Its corner stone is the surrender of per-

sonal wishes and interests to the common good, based on
the assumption that in the great essentials all lives are
a unit, and that only the excentric, accidental or circum-
stantial will have to be surrendered. Society asks these
concessions as the condition of enjoying its privileges
and protections. If any one shall prefer absolute "personal liberty," it does not object, if he will make it absolute, and carry himself off to some lone place where he
may say with Alexander Selkirk, "I am monarch of all
I survey," but to remain in society and set up this claim
is a monstrous absurdity that can never be tolerated.

It must be observed that this distinction
between the individual and society is purely one of
thought, and that it does not exist in fact, because the
individual is a part of society. In an ideal way we may
hold up the individual apart from society to consider
his peculiarities or his personal rights that do not come
under the supervision of society, but unless we remove
him entirely from society we cannot consider him apart
from it, for society is made up of individuals and is
extinct the moment you lift the individuals out of it.
There are no rights or interests of society apart from
those of individuals, in its very nature it is a compact
of individuals for the government and protection of each.
It is the duty and right of society to protect the individual by such measures as it may find necessary. This
is the first ground on which we here base the right of
prohibition. It is the duty of society to protect the
individual from being deceived and infected with this
appetite, which destroys by an illusion, and kills by an
exhilaration in which there seems a promise of more
abundant life. History contains a terrible record covering a period of three thousand years, of unsuspecting

boys who began tampering with strong drink, over whom its influence daily grew stronger, in whose lives it wrought unutterable mischief, who in later life bitterly cursed it and lamented their conduct without being able to free themselves from its influence, and whose friends recognize it as the source of all their evils. In taking account of this state of things, society must feel itself charged with the safety of the individuals of which it is composed, and recognize it as a first duty to protect the young from such a destroyer, by forbidding it to set foot upon its territory.

The second ground on which prohibition is maintained as consistent with true personal liberty is, that society owes protection to all the individuals of which it is composed, and cannot, therefore, allow one to pursue a course of conduct that will be highly injurious to many. I claim, on the ground of personal liberty, the right to walk the street unmolested and to lie down and sleep in safety, in neither of which am I secure if the open saloon is allowed in my neighborhood. Society is bound to protect and defend the personal rights and safety of its members, and to prohibit whatever puts them in peril. Wherever the sacred name of liberty is enshrined in the national constitution or in the political customs of a people it is with these limitations. Liberty is the unrestrained privilege to do right. In the most perfect freedom there is the most absolute prohibition of what is found to be injurious to society. The thief only asks personal liberty to take what he pleases, the murderer to strike down whom he likes, the pirate to seize all the vessels he can, and the drinker to put himself under the influence of rum, and allow lawless passion and wild frenzy to do their worst,

It is a falsehood in the sacred name of liberty, a black device of hell dressed in the garb of heaven. The custom in all civilized countries has been to limit personal liberty as the good of society may require. This is clearly indicated in the laws concerning the abatement of a nuisance, by which society has sought to protect itself from such evils as the saloon. A "nuisance is that which annoys or gives trouble and vexation; that which is offensive or noxious. A *liar* is a nuisance to society." "It is a settled principle that a man may himself remove a private nuisance (3 Blackstone 5) provided he causes no riot by it; a public nuisance is to be removed by process of law." The laws define the rights of the individual and of society under this point as follows:

"A man's building his house so near to mine that his roof overhangs my roof; erecting a house or other building so near to mine that it obstructs my ancient lights and windows; keeping noisome animals so near to the house of another that the stench of them incommodes him, and makes the air unwholesome; a setting up and exercising an offensive trade, as a tanner's or a tallow-chandler's; erecting a smelting-house for lead so near to the land of another that the vapor and smoke kill his corn and grass, and damage his cattle; and so to stop or divert water that uses to run to another's meadow or mill, or to corrupt or poison a water-course, by erecting a dye-house or lime-pit for the use of trade in the upper part of the stream, is a nuisance which society has a right to abate.—3 Blackstone 217, 218. "So clearly," says the great author of the 'Commentaries on the Laws of England,' "does the law of England enforce that excellent rule of Gospel morality, of doing to others as we would they should do unto ourselves." And so the same great writer, in another place, says: "All disorderly inns, or ale houses, bawdy houses, gaming houses, stage-plays, unlicensed booths and stages for rope-dancers, mountebanks, and the like, are public nuisances."—4 Blacks. 167. So lotteries have often been declared public nuisances, and have been suppressed by law as such; and so the selling of fireworks and squibs, or throwing them about in the street, is a nuisance—4 Blacks. 168. On these principles, our own commentator on American law says: "The Government may, by general regulations, interdict such uses of property as would create nuisances, and become dangerous to the lives, or health, or peace, or comfort of the citizens. Unwholesome trades, slaughter houses, operations offensive to the senses, the deposit of powder, the building with combustible materials, and the burial of the dead, may be interdicted by law, in the midst of dense masses of population, on the general and rational principle that every person ought so to use his property as not to injure his neighbors, and that private interest must be made subservient to the general interest of the community."— 2 Kent 340.

It is clear, therefore, that personal liberty is not infringed by prohibiting the saloon.

This plea for personal liberty takes yet another form. It is said that every man has a right to choose for himself what he will eat and drink, that it is tyranny to attempt to control this matter by law. There is a great outcry against "sumptuary legislation." This is a deceptive play upon words. Strong drink, as obtained at the saloon, is not used as a food, it is not taken at the time or place of taking the ordinary meal, nor for the purpose for which food is taken. It is used as a dissipation, as a pleasure drink, and as a concomitant of low vices, with which it is in eternal league, and not as a food. If the saloon, and the habit of treating, were out of the way, and if these drinks were used only at the regular meal, the evils of intemperance would be so reduced as to leave but little room for the argument for prohibition. It is not "sumptuary legislation" to enact laws for the control of a demoralizing and hurtful dissipation. It is a most glaring absurdity to call a law against the saloon an effort to determine what people shall eat and drink, simply another sly attempt on the part of this old wolf to put on sheep's clothing. Laws determining what people shall eat and wear have always been justly condemned by freemen, but laws to control vice have been condemned only by the vicious classes.

But it is regarded by some as a matter justifying grave complaint that our proposition, in addition to closing the saloon, which they grant to be a good thing, also cuts off the bottle of wine from the dinner table. No one pretends that taking wine as a part of the regular meal, is to be compared with the common saloon drinking, either as to the formation of an abnormal appetite for strong drinks, or as to its demoralizing influences. But that it does have in some cases the effect of creating an ungovernable and destructive appetite, and that this result is the more probable where the saloon exists, is equally clear, and justifies the extreme measure we propose. It is fair to estimate that, in this country, with our peculiar customs, one in a thousand of those who use wine at table are in the end destroyed by it, and no one can determine beforehand in whom the fatal effects will appear. If any other article of food should be found to contain a poisonous property that took effect in only one in a thousand of all who used it, and that no remedy for the effects could be found, and no rules laid down by which to determine in whom the deadly virus would assert itself, no prohibitory law would be necessary to protect the tables of the land from such an article. Its use at table is strongly intrenched in the social habits of the better classes, but for reasons that are not above suspicion. It is supported by custom, running back to the early ages of the world's history, and a proposition to cast it out now seems like proposing to pull out the teeth of the centuries. It is regarded as a delicious luxury, to which those who can afford it are entitled, especially as its stimulating effects are thought to aid digestion, and thus give opportunity for a larger indulgence of the appetites, and thus we find it associated in history with all feasting and demoralizing fleshly indulgences. In this country its use is in many places accepted as one of the indications of social rank and style of life, and to many people this makes it almost omnipotent. But no reason for its use can be found that can stand for a moment as an argument in justification of it in presence of the terrible effects of strong drink. There are good men, however, who still fall back on their "personal liberty," and demand their "rights." They would stop the efforts for the extirpation of the terrible saloon evil, to save their bottle of wine for the dinner table. They say this does neither them nor their neighbor harm, and we have no right to prohibit it. There may seem to be an infringement of personal rights, but not to as great an extent as is constantly practised in other matters that have the universal consent of intelligent people. If contagion has been carried into our port by an incoming vessel, every vessel that

6

enters the bay must pause at quarrantine, though there
be no sickness on board and no sign of contagious
disease, and though the delay may occasion you heavy
financial loss, or deny you the last words of a sick friend
you are hastening to meet, you must submit to quarrantine, and society says it is right.   A fire may be sweep-
ing through a city. Society has prohibited conflagra-
tions, but to carry out the prohibition may require that
your house be pulled down to stop the course of the
flames; society says it is right.   Society has prohibited
rebellion, but to enforce it, may require it to come into
your house, take your only boy, put a musket into his
hand, and march him to the battle field, where he shall
be shot down; society says it is right.   It is impossible
to accomplish the great good that society aims at, without levying a tax in the interest of its work upon those
who are to be benefited by it, and if that tax is the glass
of wine at the dinner table, it does not seem to be a
demand of such gravity as to justify going over and
joining the forces of the enemy that is fighting against
it.   Personal liberty must in all cases be subordinate to
the public good.

CHAPTER VIII.

REFORMATION BY LAW.

IS it to be expected that a prohibitory law will make an end of all crime and wickedness, and usher in the golden age, which the old Greeks said once existed, and which Christian faith declares is yet to appear on the earth? Do not our temperance advocates sometimes seem to teach that prohibition is a "short cut" out of all vices into all virtues, that there is little else worth striving for, and little more needed for the complete regeneration of society. Our opponents, at least, are glad to represent us in such an extreme position, and then to point out the absurdity of the claim with pungent sarcasm and unanswerable argument. They say: "Do not our temperance friends understand that true reformation is a great and Divine work not to be affected by human legislation, but by the influence of Divine grace in the soul? Do they not know that it is impossible to legislate men into good character, to plant the virtues in human hearts by resolutions of convention, or by act of legislature to transform demons into saints?" Yea, dear brethren, we know it very well, but we are glad to have you on high moral ground pleading for true human reformation, and we would like you to retain your position and let us hear a little further from you. You have told us that it is impossible to make men virtuous by statute, that the clerk of the legislature can not transfer men's names to the book of life—a fact we knew very well before you announced it—your argument upon it is what interests us; you say: " It is impossible to make men temperate by statute, therefore abolish the statute requiring it." The logic seems good until it is tried, then it is found wanting. Please apply your principle to other questions in life and see how it will work. It is impossible to make men honest by statute, therefore abolish the statute against theft, forgery and highway robbery. It is impossible to make men truthful by statute, therefore abolish the statute against perjury. It is impossible to make men virtuous by statute, therefore abolish the law against adultery. Laws against murder will not make saints of assassins, therefore abolish them. You cannot make men honest, temperate, or Christian by statute, therefore annul your penal codes, dismiss your officers of justice, pull down your jails and penitentiaries, level your court houses to the ground, remove the locks and bolts from your doors, let your banks and safes stand open night and day, and turn society over to the preachers and moral teachers. This logic would break up the whole fabric of society, it is at war with every human interest, and is the doctrine enthusiastically proclaimed in all dens of wickedness, where bad men combine and plot against the peace and virtue of society. It is opposed to the teachings of history and of common sense, and to the established order of all civilized nations, and even of savage tribes, the special pleading of a bad cause poor in moral character as in ideas, making desperate efforts to blind the eyes of its antagonists by thus raising a cloud of dust behind which it hopes to escape.

In every age and land criminals have inveighed

against the law as unreasonable and unjust. The thief
will say: "Nothing is clearer, you cannot make men
honest by law, if a man wants to steal he will steal, why,
then, have a law against theft? How unreasonable to
attempt to control such a matter by law? Preach and
write against theft, educate the people, establish churches
and schools, show the people the wickedness of theft, if
you need money we will help you, but don't try to control it by law." The thief knows very well that if his
advice is accepted, while the preaching is going on he
will have ample opportunity to empty the pockets of
the pious listeners. From all the lock-ups and jails, and
from all depraved classes a united chorus comes up in
favor of moral suasion and against legal prohibition.
These bloated, scared, putrescent multitudes declare
themselves, unalterably opposed to the vices that infest
society; they are shocked that people should do
such things, and are in favor of puttingan end to
the evil doing as soon as possible, but they are
unanimously of the opinion that it cannot be done by
legal prohibition, but that moral suasion is the cure.
Preach, pray, warn and entreat the people to turn from
their wickedness, but do not be guilty of the folly of
attempting to coerce them.

    Does Satan need anyone to expound this Gospel for
him? Is it not sufficiently plain to everyone? He
knows and everyone else knows that this would give
him almost undisputed possession of the field. Human
government is as truly a Divine institution as the church,
and is co-ordinate with it in the formation of character
and in the ordering of society. It accomplishes many
things impossible to the church, without which the
work of the church could not be done, and while it is

true that it cannot restore men to good character, it is equally true that little could be done to that end without it. A derrick cannot lift a block of stone to its place in the wall, neither can the laborer without the derrick, but both together can. Many things are impossible to any one agency, and are equally impossible to all others without the aid of that one. God has given us the family, civil government and the church for the perfecting of human society, and each is important in its place.

The law may not create good character, but it may be to the intelligence and conscience a rule of action by which good character may be developed. Civil law is one of the greatest unconscious educating forces of society. It is a declaration of right and duty, made manifest to the intelligence by all the means adopted for its enforcement, and for the punishment of its transgressors. Prisons, court houses, police officers and officers of the law are a constant standing announcement of law, justice and right. Thus the character grows, as the vine to the oak, supported and guided by a formal official declaration of the public conscience touching human duty.

It also aids in the formation of character by putting restraint upon the evil, and giving encouragement to the virtuous tendencies in human nature. In the growth of character moral influences are often very nearly balanced, a little added will turn the scale this way or that. The law of the land may be that deciding force. It is useless to say that men ought to be above the need of such influences. This is but to mock our poor human nature, which, as matter of fact, needs to be met at a low point by strong helping hands, and supported by all possible influences, till it has time to get strength into its ankle bones, and learn how to balance itself that it may finally walk and run in the ways of righteousness.

It is often matter of experience in recovering fallen men, that lower motives must be employed for a time till the way is prepared for the higher. In the religious life many take the first steps simply because possessed of an awful fear of perdition, but this motive having led them over the first stage of the soul's return to God, gives place to other higher motives that come into being in the process of the new birth. If a man accustomed to using strong drink were placed down in a prohibition community, he might for a time experience great inconvenience, might resist the limitations put upon him, and refrain from drinking if at all only because he could not help himself. But this enforced temperance would give reason time to get on to its feet, would show the will that appetite could be denied, and there would then be a chance for his recovery. A prohibitory law may not create good character, but it drives the enemy out, whose presence renders it impossible, and thus allows the Divine creative forces to come in and do their work.

But there are men of exalted character and astute intellect who oppose prohibition because in itself it does not work this transformation of character. If these gentlemen were passing through a region infested by cut throats, would they employ this objection against the laws prohibiting murder? They would probably wait at least till they reached the end of their journey. The law against murder does not make bad men saints, but it does restrain some men from evil till other forces have an opportunity to make them good men, besides at the same time affording a very comfortable sense of security to the community. Prohibitionists never proposed to substitute their theories for the plan of salvation, nor even for moral suasion, or public discussion and agitation. The efforts of our antagonists to put us in that absurd position, and then show the people how ridiculous we are, is one of the enforced shifts a bad cause must make when arguments are not at hand with which to meet a resolute foe. Suppose prohibition does not make bad men saints. Who has said that it would? That it would suppress much evil and put many men in a better position to be elevated and moulded by moral influences, must be clear to all who have attentively considered these pages, and this justifies its adoption.

But it is further declared that a prohibitory law would work toward a demoralization of the public, for it would not be enforced, and would simply afford an example of disobedience to law, than which nothing can be more demoralizing. These objectors take for granted the very thing that is not true, as is shown in a subsequent chapter, when they assert that a prohibitory law cannot be enforced. Even if the truth of their premise be conceded, the conclusion does not follow. The law is the announcement of the rule of righteousness, and it should be pure, no matter what the practice of the people may be, in the hope that by its educating influence society may be brought up to its high plane. Is it true that the truth must be concealed, lest men reject it and thereby be made worse? Have we reached the point where success is the test of virtue? Is a law that men will not obey to be put aside for one that pleases them? If so, what becomes of eternal righteousness? It is better to float the banner of truth where no man will stand by it, than to run up something else that will meet approval and win applause. While the law remains pure, there is a foothold for reform; if the law is corrupt, there is little ground of hope for purity of life, for the stream is poison at the fountain. The most flagrant example of the existence of law perpetually violated, is in the case of the Divine law, yet our objectiors would hardly go so far as to claim that society is demoralized by the existence of the Bible, and that it ought, therefore, to be destroyed.

Without following these objections further, which in their curious windings and twistings take yet other strange forms, this phase of the question may be dismissed with the assertion for which this chapter furnishes the argument, that if reformation cannot be affected it may be greatly aided by law.

CHAPTER IX.

MORAL AND LEGAL SUASION.

IT is not necessary to argue the right of moral suasion, for upon this point all agree. The friends of
the liquor traffic have no objection to it, and will even
advocate it as a substitute for legal suasion. It is so
amiable in character, so gentle in methods, so easily disposed of by a resolute nature, and so slow in its achievements, if unsupported by the strong arm of the law, that
few find any occasion to object to it. Prohibitionists
are met with very earnest appeals for moral suasion.
They are reminded that it is impossible to reform men
from without, that the true method is to work within, on
the conscience, the moral nature, and the intelligence.
That we must respect men's freedom of will, appeal to
their nobler nature, put them upon their honor, and
not attempt to bind them by legal cords as slaves to any
course of life, however noble. It is asserted that we
degrade and demoralize men, by the attempt to force
high moral standards upon them by act of the legislature. This argument seems very plausible in theory,
but it is a little amusing to see the friends of this horrid
traffic, the source of the great demoralization so preva-
lent in some grades of civilized society, advocating such
a lofty plane of moral action, and inveighing against
the demoralizing influence of an attempt to reform people by law. The worst characters in the community are

those who have the most exalted and impractical ideal
of Christian life, an ideal that leads them contemptu-
ously to reject as hypocrites all the humble, God-fearing
people, who in weakness are endeavoring to please the
Lord by daily obedience to his commands. No; they
will accept no such miserable living as this, they will
have ideal perfection on a magnificent scale, or they will
have nothing, and as a consequence of such logic, they
remain in the depths of iniquity. Human nature is
prone to extremes; it will pass from one extreme to
its opposite at a single bound without stopping to consider the steps it takes, and it is natural, therefore, to find
the friends of the saloon presenting us a plan of moral
reform, clear beyond the reach of ordinary mortals, and
wholly unsuited to the condition of the world as it is.
If all men were ideally perfect, then moral suasion alone
would be a reasonable theory, but taking society as it
is, it amounts to a shrewd plea for the destroyer. The
advocates of prohibition do not undervalue or neglect
moral suasion, but they insist that to be effective it must
be sustained by legal suasion. Neither, by itself, can
bring about the great reform for which we are laboring,
but the two, by the blessing of God, can and will do it.

Moral suasion we have, and we now ask for the added
strength of legal suasion. To give weight to our asking,
let us state plainly what we hope to accomplish by a
prohibitory law. It would give moral suasion a fair
field, which it now has not. While men are besotted
with strong drink, their passions inflamed and their
moral natures crushed, there is little hope for moral suasion. If, however, you can lift the man to his feet, get
him from under the power of the charmer long enough
for reason to clear up, and for conscience to begin to act,

there will be a chance to restore him to manhood. It is the common-sense method of putting up your fences to keep the flocks out before you sow your fields. This is the plan on which civilized society has proceeded in all countries. It enacts laws prohibiting theft, murder, adultery, and a long list of crimes; not for a moment supposing that these laws will amend the moral nature of the citizen so that he will have no impulse to wrong doing, but that it may accomplish the other useful purpose of holding the criminally disposed in check through fear, till moral suasion has opportunity to reach the intelligence and the conscience, and effect the desired moral change. The vices would utterly destroy society, and moral suasion have no field at all for action, were they not held in check by the law. In this respect the law is to society what the fence is to the field. In presenting the case thus it is not claimed that all drinking is a crime as theft is, but that its aggravated forms with which we are chiefly dealing is not only a crime, but the mother of crime. The milder forms show a constant tendency to run into the aggravated forms, therefore we would prohibit the whole business, forbid the stream and close up the fountain till society gets its brain clear and its character rectified, and is prepared to make an impartial judgment concerning it.

Another thing we should accomplish would be to stop at once a great part of the drinking that now prevails. We should not stop it all. Our opponents say truly, for they know their men and the grip they have on them, that it is impossible to stop drinking entirely. That there is a class of drinkers who will have rum at any cost, we have seen till our hearts are sick with the spectacle. In every city these devotees are to be found, men who lay on the altar of Bacchus all that the heart has to give, and curse the poverty, which forbids them to give more. They give money, they give health, they give reputation, they give home, they give wife and children, they damn their souls and damn their posterity that they may have rum. They will have it, they would leap into hell to get it, and they do transform earth into hell by making and using it. But this class is comparatively small and will be very short lived, it will soon burn out. Prohibition can do but little for these poor victims, it has come too late for them. Unless God's mercy interposes, there is nothing left for them but to rush into the open mouth of hell not far away.

But the great body of drinkers are not of this class, though they may be moving toward it. They drink for good fellowship because invited by a friend, because weary or worn, supposing it may help them, casually because it is near and convenient. If there were no invitation to step into an open door, or if it were six blocks away, a great part of the casual drinking that is preparing its victims for the hopeless state of which I have spoken, would at once cease. A prohibitory law, by removing the saloon from the street, would take away opportunity and temptation.

It would also remove temptation from the boys. There are ten million boys in this country just stepping out into the world, eager, buoyant, spirited fellows, ambitious to see and know the world, ready to enter any open door, prompt to try anything that promises pleasure or fun, confiding in anyone who proposes to show them something new, swarming up and down the streets, past these man-traps that are specially anxious to catch the sons of wealthy and respectable parents. In God's

name, are these boys to be exposed to this peril, with
the moral certainty that five hundred thousand of them
will become drunkards, and no man lift his hand to blot
out these sinks of iniquity? Can any one look on the
spectacle and not feel every noble impulse of his nature
urging him to the rescue? Argument about it seems
preposterous, there is but one course open to any man
who will look at this spectacle till he comprehends its
meaning, unless he is dead to every noble impulse. Ten
million boys in the street before the open saloon, means
that five hundred thousand of them at least will become
drunkards. The man who can stop in the presence of
the spectacle to quibble about his glass of wine for
dinner, or about personal liberty, or the probable effec-
tiveness of moral suasion, ought to be headed toward
the rear of the reformer's camp, and marched at double
quick to the music of the "rogue's march," till far
enough away never again to be found in company for
which he was not worthy. Systematic efforts are made
to entrap these boys. A saloon keeper stood leaning
against his window casing looking out at the falling rain.
It was a dark day and business was not good. One
customer was loitering away the time in the saloon,
occasionally exchanging remarks with the man at the
window. Presently the saloon keeper tapped on the
window, and with a smile beckoned to some one without
to come in. The door opened and a bright, well-dressed
boy on his way from school entered. The saloon keeper
said to him: "My boy, would you not like a glass of
lemonade?" "Yes sir, thank you," the boy replied.
The saloon keeper made as good a glass of lemonade as
he could and gave it to the boy. As the boy was leaving the saloon keeper said to him: "Now, when you want

some more lemonade come in and I will be glad to prepare it for you." When the door closed the man sitting
by said: "What did you do that for?" "Oh, business,"
was the reply. "Yes," said the man ; "but I don't see
how there was any business in that, you did not charge
him anything for it." The saloon keeper said : "You
don't know who that boy is; do you see that splendid
house across the hill? That is Col. Jones' residence, he
is very wealthy and this is his only son. That boy has
been taught to believe that the saloon is the gate to hell.
He will go away to-day saying to himself, 'there is some
mistake about this, that is not such a bad place?' He
will come again some day, and I will give him another
glass of lemonade. After awhile I will put a little of
something into the lemonade, and he will soon form an
appetite for something stronger, then I've got him, and
I'll get the property." A prohibitory law proposes to
sweep these agents of the bottomless pit from the street,
and to give the boys a chance for life.

Such a law would make it difficult and disreputable to
drink, for no man could drink without consorting with
law breakers, and incurring the odium attaching to such
associations. This would, in time, if not at once, put an
end practically to drunkenness. Those who are not
already under the spell of the charmer are not going to
hunt for it in subterranean hiding places, or expose themselves to arrest and prosecution and loss of social standing for the privilege of experimenting with a glass
of whiskey. I speak of this the more confidently
because my college days were spent in a college
town where prohibition existed, and there was not a
place in the town where liquors were sold. A drunken
man was hardly ever seen, a drunken student was never

known, and I have no knowledge of one of that body of students who has since become a drunkard.

There is a more selfish phase of this question not unworthy of mention. We should secure protection to our property and persons by a prohibitory law. The whole community goes to sleep every night with dynamite in the cellar, and a lot of half crazed men playing with it—fit conduct only for a set of fools. If we are not blown to fragments before morning, it is not because of any precaution, wisdom, virtue, or courage on our part. We know that the accursed thing surrounds us on every hand, and that at any moment we may be its victim. It is only a mercy of heaven that we have been permitted to escape till now. Every day brings tidings of "the destruction that wasteth at noon day" and at midnight as well. A baptismal party returning from church through the streets of Brooklyn passed a saloon just as a row occurred within. In the carriage sat the mother with the babe at her breast which she had just consecrated to God, happy in the consciousness of having fulfilled her duty to the child. A pistol ball from the saloon penetrated the child's head and through it into the mother's body and both lay dead, victims of the saloon. There is no highway secure, no private walk safe, no hiding place where it may not find you, no foot of soil beyond its reach while allowed the freedom of the land. We have a right to ask protection from such perils. Government is instituted for the purpose of protecting the lives, property and liberties of the citizens. No government discharges these functions fully that allows such a destroyer as the saloon, and such a menace to liberty as it is, to exist.

CHAPTER X.

CHARACTER.

ARBITRARY prohibition is tyranny. There is general consent to the prohibition of that which works evil to society, but human nature revolts against it, if adopted without reason, in the interests of a class, a monopoly, or for the benefit of those enacting it. To be successful it must rest upon the broad ground of the public good, not as interpreted by radical reformers, visionary idealists, or impracticable fanatics, but as understood by the great body of the community in relation to financial, social, intellectual, moral and religious progress. Puritanical theorists, and religionists of exalted character and ideals, might to their own reason justify the adoption of prohibition, where it would neither be wise in policy nor right in principle as an act of government. The prohibition of a great traffic can be justified to the common intelligence only on the ground that it is bad in character, injurious in its effects, and detrimental to the interests of the community. The preceding pages present considerations that seem to be sufficient to justify the extirpation of the liquor traffic, but I wish here to look a little more closely at the character of the thing itself as a justification of this measure. *It is a law-breaker.* It lives in the habitual violation of law, ignores, boldly defies it, and is in league and fraternity with all law-breakers. The laws against selling to minors, to intoxicated persons, after certain hours of

7

the day, on the holy Sabbath, and many others, it treats with utter contempt. It is a constant standing example of lawlessness, educating and inciting the worst classes of the community to the disregard of all law by the ease with which it tramples upon its requirements, and controls the officers appointed to enforce it. The gentlemen who are so fearful of the demoralizing effect of a prohibitory law that fails of absolute enforcement, in educating the community to lawlessness by the spectacle of such a failure to enforce law, until they have such a real case over which to shed their tears, might here find a cause entirely worthy of the pent up floods of their moral indignation against the demoralization of society by an example of lawlessness.

But looking a little deeper, we find that it has most resolutely set itself to the work of corrupting the very source of law. It boldly marches into the halls of legislation, jingling the gold gotten in its nefarious business, and lays it on the altar of justice at which the representatives of the people have sworn fidelity to God and the interests of the community, and for a price much larger than Judas received secures the betrayal of the Son of God and of the interest of humanity, by men who go about the business with a traitorous kiss in the form of a license law or some vaunted restrictive measure. It is a terrible fact in our political history, prophetic of coming disasters that involve the breaking down of our whole social and political fabric, a fact so clear, so open, so often repeated that none can doubt its existence, that the worst moral elements of the community are able deliberately to buy for money or political influence the sworn legislative conscience of the American people. They even go back of the legislature, and to the hard working, ignorant, poverty burdened, partially informed voter, who knows little of what is at stake, offer the tempting inducement of a bank note for his vote. It poisons the primary fountains of justice and truth, debauches conscience in the original sources of law, corrupts the whole stream of political action, and when it has secured the enactments it sought, places its foot on the neck of the patient public, and brandishes its blood-stained weapons in the air. If defeated at other points it marches into court and fights and barters with all courage and cunning craft, to defeat the claims of justice. Testimonies, statistics and facts in support of these positions lie about us in various forms of publication till we weary looking at them.

Our argument is that such a law-breaker ought to be sent to the Dry Tartugas, to the infernal regions whence it came, or anywhere out of the great republic, whose very existence it endangers. It has earned the deadly hate and the uncompromising hostility of every pure minded man and intelligent patriot.

I furthermore allege against this traffic as a reason for its prohibition, *that it is a thief.* I have already shown that it every year takes out of the pockets of the people of this country $1,000,000,000, for which it makes no adequate return. It does this in the first case by deception and stealth, in the last by force. The thief may with great dexterity thrust his hand into your pocket and take your gold, leaving you none the worse save for your loss. He may open your door while you sleep, and by stealth secure valuable treasure, leaving you in the peaceful slumber which kind nature gives. Or, he may stand before you with an enticing liquid, that pleases the appetites, inflames the passions and wins

your money, while concealed beneath these outward
attractions he gives you in return disease and death.
At first the purchaser believes he is buying pleasure—
go look on him after the article of his purchase has had
its full effect in a course of ten years use, and answer
me, is it not a most cruel and tremendous deception?
a deception practiced for the purpose of obtaining money
under its false pretence. I will be just to the venders
of strong drink, and concede that many of them are kind
and humane in feeling, they regret the terrible effects of
drunkenness, they would gladly obliterate all the evils
of intemperance if they could do it without interfering
with their business, but they must make their business
a success whatever stands or falls. This is the open
secret of the whole case, they appeal to the appetites of
the people and offer them pleasure for money, they get
the money and give cursing and death.

When the process of alcoholizing is somewhat
advanced the deception takes another form. The great
reserve force of moderate drinkers, from which the dare-
devil army of drunkards is constantly replenished, finds
in itself this experience. If it neglects its usual pota-
tions, great languor and depression incapacitating for any
prolonged or vigorous activity results. A return to the
stimulating cup restores the vanished vigor, and labor
becomes a pleasure. This is a demonstration in a scientific way, by experience, that strong drink is necessary
to maintain a good working condition. Many men
reason with themselves thus: "The temperance argument
seems good, the evils of drinking are truly great, but I
am so constituted that I cannot get on without my regular glass, which I take without excess, and which I
find as necessary as my meals. Only yesterday, after

reading an earnest plea for total abstinence, I thought I would do without my morning stimulant, and as a result I was weak, nervous and unsteady in all my work and nothing went right. At noon I took my usual stimulant and in half an hour I was myself, and had no trouble the rest of the day. I have often made the trial with the same result in every case, and this demonstrates to me that whatever may be true for others, I am so constituted that I must have it." This course of reasoning and the experience on which it is based will be found only in the man who is already pretty thoroughly alcoholized. That is, in the man whose system has been so brought under the influence of these stimulants that it will not endure to be deprived of them without a mighty protest in the form of a refusal to work until the old regime is restored. It establishes no truth, but that this man has become the bond slave of this monster, that he has made it almost a necessity to himself by giving it the keys to his inner life, with power to bind and loose at pleasure. It is very poor logic, but exactly in the line of deception constantly pursued by this wily foe of the race, to attempt to apply this man's experience to the mass of men, and say that since he finds strong drink necessary to his comfort and working power, therefore all men would be better for its use. But the great mass of men have never established in themselves the condition that makes a stimulant necessary to their comfort and strength, and they can go to their daily tasks without a stimulant and with no feeling of lassitude and weakness for want of it. This continual cry that nature requires a stimulant, as proven by experience is a deception, for the simple reason that those who make it are not in a natural but in an alcoholized state, and that those who are in a natural state have no such sense of need. If we are to take testimony on this point I submit that we should hear it from those who are in a natural state, and are, therefore, in a condition to speak in an unbiased way of the demands of nature. There is also a large number who were once in the condition of those who think it necessary from long use, who have recovered themselves from its influence, and testify that when once really free from it they no longer feel the need of it. This makes plain the nature of the deception under which the patrons of this traffic are held to its support.

But in due time a point is reached where the deception is dissipated, and the unfortunate victim comes to look stern, cold reality in the face. He is compelled to see and acknowledge the delusion under which he has been rushing into the open jaws of hell, but, alas, the discovery has come too late! Deception is no longer necessary in his case, for the traffic has established such control over him that it can now use undisguised force, and compel him to the support he once was glad to give. When the alcohol habit is fully established you cannot move it by arguments, persuasion, entreaties, expostulations, bribes, threats or punishment; it has a death grip and will release its hold only with the death of its victim. Often does the unfortunate inebriate writhe, struggle, bind himself by solemn oaths, and put forth all his strength, only to be cast down to a lower depth by the demon to whom he has sold his liberties. By a force entrenched in his being, fortified behind every nerve, with batteries located in every blood vessel, and with the brain a citadel stocked with weapons and munition for a long and spirited defense, .

there is little hope left, save by the interposition of Omnipotence. This plain statement of the common facts of this traffic from which it appears that it at first uses deception and finally employs force to secure money for which it makes a return that in the end proves worse than nothing, justifies the assertion that it is a thief.

More than this, I allege that *it is a murderer.* The article it exposes to public sale as a pleasure drink, contains deadly poison in such quantities as not to be clearly perceptible in its effects by common drinkers, and yet sufficient in amount to produce death in a great number of cases. It is estimated that 100,000 people die in this country annually at the hands of this blood-stained traffic. It does not relieve the case at all, that this traffic does its work by the administration of a narcotic that deadens the pain, pleases and delights the victim, lifts him up with an exhilaration in which he thinks himself enriched with a double portion of life and vigor, and that his death is reached by slow stages under various disguises that leave him entirely unconscious of the process that is going forward.

In this death mingle and blend all the horrors of deepest shade that have ever darkened this beautiful world. The savage of the plains, who bound his victim, and filled his flesh with splinters of wood saturated with oil and then set fire to them, made but a clumsy, feeble attempt at torture as compared with the long-drawn, far reaching, shrewdly devised and terribly effective methods of this colossal savage of civilization. Poor Prometheus, chained to the rocks with the vultures at his liver, scarcely seems to be an object of pity in comparison with these victims of the liquor traffic. Look at the process of torture. When the subject is well under the influence of the narcotic, this monster begins by smearing his pride of character and self-respect with the slime and filth of the pit till he becomes loathsome in his own eyes. Then he drives him upon vile, coarse, brutal conduct till he alienates his friends, and turns love to hate and admiration to loathing for him. Then he thrusts red hot bolts through and through conscience and moral affections, and leaves them to writhe and die in agony. He hamstrings the love of money and then lashes it with whips of flame to make it use its remaining powers in his behalf. With red hot pincers he pulls out by the roots all natural affections and drops into the wounds the bitter gall of hell. In every ganglion of the brain he lodges a demon to keep alive the fierce conflagration of appetite that is consuming him. He thrusts a poisoned arrow into every nerve and vital organ, and leaves it there to fester and spread disease through the body. He drops liquid fire into every blood vessel, and when the poor wretch bursts into conflagration holds him aloft in his hand like a burning torch to show his power, and at last throws the charred remnant into the gutter as a thing too vile for even his blood-stained hand. Let civilization write over his brow *murderer* and send him forth in his true character, or banish him to the regions whence he came.

It is a co-partner with all vices and crimes. There is not a vice that does not find, in the liquor traffic, a strong ally and a powerful support. The saloon is a school of vice, where the vicious classes congregate and by mutual interaction stimulate each other to vile deeds, where plots are laid, passions aroused, and resolution acquired, and whence the men go forth, whose deeds are a terror to the community, and a reproach to our civilization. Thieves, house-breakers, roughs, prostitutes, murderers, and all vile classes move about the saloon as a common center, back into which all their bad blood flows that it may be re-charged with the spirit of evil and returned to them. In all the haunts of base men and bad women strong drink is high priest and chief lord. Where dark schemes are to be devised, and fiendish plots are to be set on foot, the wine-glass must lend its inspiration ere the witchery of evil will work. If a midnight deed is to be done that is to startle the dawn and fill the day with horror, chief reliance for courage and nerve is placed in the aid of this wonder-worker of evil. Often has the perpetrator of the most horrible deeds confessed that only repeated draughts of that which stimulates passion, and deadens conscience and moral feeling, enabled him to execute his fiendish designs. It is the very soul and life of the criminal classes, and, therefore, for the suppression of crime and in the interests of morality it ought to be cast out of society.

If the traffic is so bad in character, what must be said of those who engage in it? It is never wise to condemn men wholesale. No class is without exceptions to its general characters. There was a Judas among the disciples, and there may be good men among liquor sellers, though we cannot account for the one or the other being in company to which they are so unlike. Some are brought up in the business, or become committed to it by circumstances over which they seem to have no control, and they remain in it with a constant protest in their hearts against it, waiting a convenient opportunity to escape from it. There are many such who abhor the business, but for this very reason they are the more guilty if they continue in it. It were better to apply a match to the accursed stuff and walk out into the street a free, penniless man, than to continue in what conscience condemns as a wrong to humanity, and a sin against God.

It remains true, as the testimony of the ages teaches, that a man shows his character by the business and the associations he chooses. How can a good man choose a business the chief influence of which he knows is to demoralize men, to strengthen and stimulate the vicious classes, and to add to the sins and sufferings of the community? Is a man who sells that which he knows will make thefts and murders any better than a thief and a murderer? Can a man be better than his business? Does not his doing declare what he is and prove his character? Many of the greatest criminals have been kind, affectionate and orderly, except in the line of their criminality. It is freely granted that many liquor dealers are examples of business integrity, and of all the virtues that constitute good citizenship, but the business into which they put the strength of their lives must be accepted as determining their characters. They are doing a corrupting, murderous business, and all the seas cannot wash from their hands that dark spot.

It does not relieve the case to change the point of view from the low saloon to the elegant apartments of the wholesale dealer. This is simply following the stream toward the fountain, rising to a grade of higher intelligence and greater responsibility in the deadly business. When the wholesale dealer ships his barrels of liquor, he knows it is to go into the glasses of the retail dealers, into the throats of drinkers, and spend itself at last in suffering and sorrow in the homes of the people. From manufacturer to retail dealer, all are under the curse of doing the devil's business as the high priests of his kingdom in demoralizing men, and in transforming this beautiful world into a howling pandemonium, and whatever approval or reward they may expect must be from him.

It has been insisted that if our measure of prohibition is adopted, it should be with a provision to compensate dealers and manufacturers for the loss of business and property they would sustain by its enforcement. This is never demanded in behalf of pirates, burglars, counter-feiters, or any other class who prey upon the public, and why should it be here? Because, it is said, the public encouraged these men to go into this business by making it lawful, and by guaranteeing protection to it. This reasoning has force, but does not seem conclusive, espe-cially when we remember that this guarantee of protec-tion was, in most cases, at least, obtained by bribery, or by cunning political manœuvers, that defeated the real will of the people. This business has employed its immense wealth and political influence to corrupt legis-lative action, and to secure guarantees that it knew the people would not approve. In this case it would hardly appear that the people 'are morally responsible, and should, therefore, share with the liquor dealers the loss entailed by prohibition.

Painful as it may be to see the property of any wrested from their hands, it is much more painful to see it used in spreading abroad the desolations of the liquor traffic. The aggressive attitude which the venders of strong drink have assumed, throws a strong light on the question of character. There was a time when men were content to offer their liquors for sale and await the com-ing of customers. But there is now more enterprise in the business. Organizations, for aggression and defense, have been formed, extending from manufacturer to retail dealer, and their power is being felt from ocean to ocean and from the lakes to the gulf. These organizations include all branches of the business, but Mr. D. R. Locke, a most competent authority, gives such a graphic account of the particular efforts made for the extension of the lager beer business, that I will content myself with quoting from him on this branch of the business alone. He says:

"The thirty-years-ago sellers of stimulants never made efforts to extend their business; they merely sold to those who came for drink, and who conducted themselves with as much decency as liquor permits, while boozing. Had this continued there never would have been a movement for prohibition that would have had the strength of a straw.

"But the nature of the business has changed entirely within thirty years. The introduction of lager-beer opened a field for money-making so illimitable as to stimulate the cupidity of the more eager seekers after money. Lager-beer was originally a seductive fluid, a mild-mannered demon, as innocent in appearance as spring water, and as beautiful. There are but few things on earth more beautiful than lager-beer. The rich color in the glass, the liquid itself as clear as water, with its delicate amber tint, surmounted with the creamy foam overtopping it, is a very pretty sight, and one which appeals strongly to the lust of the eye. And then its taste! The delicate, sweetish bitter is wonderfully grateful, and, when cold as ice, the taste lingers lovingly on the palate, the warmth cheers the stomach, and it is as refreshing a drink as man could wish. And in justice it must be said that the lager-beer of thirty years ago was comparatively harmless. Then it was made of nothing but malt and hops, it was "laid" for nearly a year until it had undergone all the fermentations, and it could be taken, in moderate quantities, safely. The percentage of alcohol in it was much less than now, for reasons which will be given hereafter.

"The new drink which the German brewers introduced made rapid progress in public favor. The temperance advocates of that day looked upon it without hostility, for they preferred that men should drink the mild lager rather than the more fiery whiskey or rum. Therefore, its use was rather encouraged than discouraged.

"The brewers saw in this their opportunity. They built great breweries, some of them with a capacity going a long way up into the hundreds of thousands of barrels per annum, which was not to be wondered at, as the profit on each barrel was from $1.50 to $2.00.

"Then came the very important question, how was this great volume of beer to be sold? These acute men were not long in solving that problem. They took their good hard dollars and established everywhere what is now known as the "beer-saloon." They found for them conscienceless creatures, with neither morals nor decency, who never had money enough to pay for a meal of victuals, hang-dog fellows with long mustaches, and trousers chewed off at the heels, with dirty neckties to hide still more dirty shirts, paper-collar twice-turned abominations, who would be thieves but for the lack of courage, the fellows who crawl between heaven and earth, living, the good Lord who permits them only knows how. They took this class of persons and rented for them each a room or two, and put in a counter, some

round pine tables and cheap chairs; they supplemented
a cheap pool-table and a few packs of cards, and put in
behind the bar a keg of beer, a few bottles of whiskey,
and some glasses, and set them to work—perfectly
equipped devil's missionaries.

"How could they afford to trust this property with such
men? Nothing could be more safe. They did not sell
it—it remained their property, all there was of it. The
keeper was compelled to sign an agreement to sell so
many kegs of their beer a day, as the condition of enjoying the use of the place. Of course, the beer had to be
paid for on delivery, so all the capital required was the
price of one small keg, which amounted to from $2.00 to
$2.50. In most cases the poor wretch did not have this
trifling amount, and the brewer was forced to give him
the first keg on credit. But as there are one hundred
glasses of beer in a quarter barrel, and as each glass
brings five cents, the debt was always a safe one.

"Now comes the point. This poor devil, this tool of
the brewer, has to sell so much beer a day to keep his
place. He has to pay the rent of the "saloon," for the
brewer either owns it or is responsible for it, and also he
must pay for so much beer per diem.

"This new system changed the entire nature of the
business. The retailer is no longer the quiet man engaged
in a half-disreputable business (for, in its best estate,
liquor selling has never been counted a respectable trade),
but he is a missionary for the diffusion of alcohol, and
an urgent, indefatigable fastener of the alcoholic appetite
upon just as many as he can get his unclean hands upon.
He goes out in search of customers, and by his efforts
liquor is no longer a passive nuisance, but an active,
aggressive evil.

"How does he do it? He has a thousand ways. He makes his rooms as pleasant as possible; he takes the daily newspapers, which are free to his customers; he hangs cheap but attractive pictures upon his walls—always of a demoralizing nature, for his business is to demoralize; he provides games of chance and skill for his customers, the stake being always beer; he invites workingmen to sit in his place, where there is a warm stove in the winter, and artificially cooled air in the summer; he spreads a cheap lunch which is free to all comers, the viands being invariably thirst-provoking, and all this sort of thing.

"Now, the workingman who comes into this place may have before, on occasion, taken a glass of beer, when he happened to be in the way of it, but he had no especial appetite for it, and no regular craving. Before the opening of this place in his neighborhood, he went to his home sober, and spent his evenings with his family, as a decent workingman should, and there was always bread and meat in his larder, and his wife and children were decently and comfortably clad. For the purpose of meeting his mates and discussing the current topics of the day, and for the unhealthy pleasure of playing games, he becomes very quickly habituated to frequenting the saloon, and, of course, takes his glass of beer. He must do this, for he is too proud to enjoy the facilities of the place without making some return. Sociability being the chief attraction, he is invited to drink by the other frequenters, his sense of liberality compels him to reciprocate, and so he, who dropped in for one glass, goes out with a dozen under his belt, comfortably drunk. He didn't mean to, but custom, the custom of the place, most artfully devised, forced him into it. He goes home drunk every night, after a month or two of it.

"The effect of the alcohol poison is not well enough understood. No man can touch it without fastening upon himself a craving for more. This is a physiological law which is fixed and certain. The man who comes to stopping at a place of this kind every night and taking one glass, within a week finds a half-dozen necessary. And the seller helps him along the downward road as rapidly as possible. There is always upon the counter a plate of picked codfish, or red herrings cut into proper lengths, or pretzels covered with salt, all thirst-provokers, and they actually put salt into the beer, that the desire for the pleasant liquor may be increased. Beer becomes a necessity to him before he is aware of it, and his fate is fixed. The seller can count upon so much a day from him as certainly as though he had it in his till.

"And this is not all, by any means. Lager-beer originally contained only three or four per cent. of alcohol, but it now contains ten and twelve per cent. The original beer did not make drunkards fast enough. It took too long a time to fix the habit so as to make the victim profitable. Hence they threw in glucose to make more alcohol, and all sorts of cheap drugs of the maddening kind, that the drinker might be bound hand and foot, and put into their possession in an absolutely helpless condition as soon as possible. It was not enough to make a beer-drinker of him—to get the largest profit it became necessary to *make a drunkard of him*. It resulted as anticipated. The beer-drunkard is the worst drunkard in the world, and his chains are the heaviest and strongest.

"A more infernal infernalism was never devised, and if it does not call for some sort of law, nothing does.

"But it does not stop here. Men are not the only vic-tims. There are boys in the neighborhood, striplings from thirteen to sixteen. The agent of the brewers arranges his trap for them. They have no money, so he gives them credit. He has a room for them secure from observation, in which they may play cards, or pool, or other forms of billiards; all for beer, of course.

"When the account swells to a sufficient amount he demands payment. The alarmed boy cannot pay. He frightens him with threats of appealing to his parents, and when the boy is sufficiently ground down, he sug-gests that his mother has linen, his elder brother a revolver, his father books, and his sister jewelry, and he gives him the name of a pawnbroker who will advance him all the money he wants, on articles of this kind. The frightened boy jumps at this easy escape, goods are missed from the house, servant-girls are discharged for theft, and the thing goes on until the boy becomes a confirmed thief, and so bold in his operations that dis-covery is made.

"Whether he finally gets to the House of Correction or not, he is a beer-sodden wreck before he is eighteen, and is the bond-slave of the drink-fiend forever."

"The vast brewing establishments of Milwaukee, Cin-cinnati, Toledo and Rochester have millions invested in this business, and their success in the introduction of their beer may be measured by their wealth. They are the richest corporations in the country, and no instances are known where, with fair business management, they have not amassed enormous fortunes.

"They keep energetic men travelling all the time establishing saloons. In the city of Toledo, with 90,000 population, they have 800, and the number is con-

8

stantly and rapidly increasing. A corporation cannot break ground in the subsurbs for a factory, that the brewer's agent is not there to purchase a lot upon which to erect a saloon, and the moment an addition to the city is platted, a saloon is the first building that goes up. They know every workingman, and the wages he gets, and they demand their share of it, and generally get it.

Did they confine their operations to the cities, it would not be so bad, but they do not. They have invaded the country, and there is scarcely a hamlet or cross-roads in which they are not represented. With millions of capital, with an energy that is wonderful, with all the zeal that cupidity inspires and feeds, they are everywhere. There is not a family that they do not threaten, nor one that is outside their influence.

It is this aggressive feature of the trade which has awakened a demand for the interposition of the law to prohibit, instead of restraining. Heavy taxation of the traffic has no effect, for the profits of the business are so great that no taxation has ever been reached that they could not laugh at. The profit on beer is enormous, and they have a safeguard against taxation in this, that they make their own prices and they have possession of their customers. Should a tax upon beer be made so great that the seller should be compelled to double the price, it would make no difference in sales to his regular customers. They must and will have it."

On the ground of the character, aims, methods and results of the traffic we demand that it shall be prohibited as an enemy to the public good.

CHAPTER XI.

WILL IT PROHIBIT?

THE evils of intemperance have been so many and so great, that all classes have united in demanding the adoption of laws that would regulate and restrain them. Experiments have been made upon a wide field and on a vast scale with the uniform result of finding that the traffic is hostile to all laws designed to limit its work of death, and that it will submit to none except as compelled by superior force. License laws in great variety have been tried, only to prove their impotence in dealing with such a monster evil, their provisions have been evaded or openly defied by those who dictated them and were most earnest in their advocacy. That they have failed of their object, and have been openly and persistently violated, needs no proof—it is seen and recognized by all. But it is a curious fact that in all this discussion the friends of the liquor traffic have never objected to license laws on the ground that they would fail of their object. None can be more fully informed as to the reality and extent of this failure than themselves, for it is entirely due to their cunning evasions or their bold defiance. Yet it has never occurred to them that this failure constituted a valid argument against such laws, at least they have not brought it into the discussion as an objection to their adoption. Indeed, it may not be uncharitable to suppose that the fact that these laws fail to exercise any perceptible restraint upon the evils of intemperance is the very reason they encounter so little objection from this source. If the saloon can have the authorization and protection of the law, if it is simply permitted to live though placed under heavy assessments for the public good, it will have vitality and force enough to make its way. If only allowed to live it will rend all the legal cords with which it may be bound, and Sampson-like show its power for slaying thousands undiminished. by such impediments. But the moment a prohibitory law is proposed these virtuous guardians of the public morals become strongly exercised in conscience lest something will be done to debauch the morals of the public. They lift up their prophet's voice in solemn warning, as though Nathan had risen from his grave to utter a last protest against the incoming tides of wickedness. It would set before the community an example of law breaking, since they would make it their special business to trample upon the law if enacted; it would violate the sacred rights of personal liberty, it would lead to the worst forms of deception and hypocrisy in requiring them to conduct their business in a secret way by various arts of deception, and these are such gross infractions of ideal morality as a liquor dealer's conscience can never tolerate.

They oppose a prohibitory law because it cannot be enforced. This objection throws a strong light upon the character of this business, which in its very nature is against all law, in league with all law breakers, an accomplice in all wickedness, a necessary ally in all deeds of darkness, the help in time of need to which base men and vile women always turn. Its studied deliverance and carefully considered objection to a prohibitory law is that it cannot be enforced. That is, if such a law be passed the liquor dealers declare that they will defy it, trample upon it, and avow their strength and the demoralization of the puplic to be such that the law *cannot* be enforced. Were law breakers ever more candid and insolent? Have any of our criminal classes sunk so low as to openly declare their intention to transgress the law? Is the public in such a helpless condition that outlaws combine and dictate by threats of resistance and violence the laws by which we are to be governed? Is anything further needed as a testimony to the character of the business and of the men engaged in it, than their own bold declaration of lawlessness?

But they say they are opposed to such a law because if adopted, it will not be executed, and more liquor will be sold than before, and the evils of intemperance will be increased. It is the liquor dealers who are alarmed lest prohibition should prove a failure and injure the temperance cause. Does not every man know that they are hypocrites? That if they really believe what they say, they would be the most ardent friends of prohibition? It has been their constant effort to enlarge their sales, and if prohibition gave promise of this result, the "liquor league" would not be so insane as to spend its hundreds of thousands in the effort to defeat it, as they say, "for self-protection." The Devil himself stands before us as an angel of light in the person of these objectors, and with white necktie and sanctimonious looks, lifts up his holy hands in horror, and warns his "dear temperance friends" not to injure the dear cause they love so much by adopting prohibition. They would have us preach, pray, educate public sentiment, distribute temperance literature, train the children, start crusades,—anything, so we do not commit the blunder of trying prohibition, and "disgrace the cause by dabbling in the dirty pool of politics." See these saints! They have turned temperance advocates, and propose to aid the cause by giving it the benefit of their experience, and by pointing out the perils to be encountered.

It may be accepted as a very safe rule for the friends of temperance to do just the opposite of what the liquor dealers advise, however plausible their arguments, or sanctimonious their manners. No class understands the real strongholds of the business as well as those whose capital is invested in it, and all their suggestions with reference to the control of the evils of intemperance will be framed with reference to the protection of their capital. When your enemy informs you that a certain position in his lines is well fortified, closely guarded and very strong, it will be safe for you to conclude that that is his weak point. An old colored man in Virginia, having exercised his newly conferred right of voting for three or four years, was asked if he "was able to read and keep himself posted on the political questions of the day." He answered: "No, massa, Uncle Ben not able to read." "Well, then, how do you know which way to vote if you are not able to read?" "Oh, well, Uncle Ben has no trouble 'bout dat." "Why not, how do you manage it?" "Wy, it is de easiest ting in de world. Do you know Col. Jones ober dar, what was in de rebel army?" "Yes." "Well, all I has to do is jes' watch how he votes." "Well, but you don't mean to say you vote as he does?" "Lor' bless you, no, hunney, I jes' watches how he votes, then I vote 'zactly de oder way, and I's sho to be right ebery time."

Whatever may be thought of the colored man's logic in the case before him, it is perfectly safe when applied to the teaching and the votes of the liquor dealers. Go in the opposite direction from that of the liquor league, and you will find the true temperance principles and workers. I do not at this point charge upon the "liquor league" anything more than common business shrewdness, with such tactics as naturally go with the business, and I suppose there are few people stupid enough to think them deficient in common human enterprise when such enormous gains await their efforts. Having embarked in the business, they wish to make as much out of it, and to make it as respectable as possible. Who would expect less than that from them? When they see a handwriting on the wall, in the form of a proposed prohibitory amendment, their knees smite together with fear, and immediately all the wise men and soothsayers are called to suggest some means of escaping the impending calamity. The wise men say this business has been weighed in the balances of conscience and truth, by the intelligent christian public, and found wanting; its days are numbered, and its kingdom must be destroyed. Then it is proposed that a lying prophet shall be sent out to deceive the saints, and thus protect the endangered cause. He is instructed to say: "We, the liquor league, representing the liquor dealers of the United States, are in favor of temperance, and are unalterably opposed to the evils of intemperance, and for this reason we oppose prohibition, because if adopted it would be a failure, and more liquor would be drunk than ever before, and because it would promote the worst forms of deceit and hypocrisy." Is any one so dull as to expect anything less than this of such a business so placed?

There are few indeed so blind as not to see the sophistry and downright hypocrisy of this plea, and to see in it also the highest possible endorsement of the wisdom of prohibition. No one so well as the enemy can tell what weapon hurts most.

Serious argument of the question of the possible enforcement of prohibition seems to be no longer necessary, and, indeed, would not be attempted after the splendid achievements of the past few years, were it not for the constant, persistent misrepresentation of the facts.

A surface view shows that there is nothing the liquor dealers fight against so earnestly, and the temperance people contend for so persistently, as prohibition. What does this mean? Are both sides in error? Are the whiskey men fighting against their own interests? Are temperance people contending for a measure that would prove the overthrow of their hopes, and this after a fair trial in many fields? Are the shrewd men on both sides smitten with blindness? He who decides that all men are fools, thereby gives the best evidence that he himself is the biggest fool of all. It is fair to assume that both temperance and anti-temperance men have common shrewdness and logical acumen, and know for what they are contending.

We are not left to conjecture, nor to the "dim light of reason's fitful ray" on this subject. Prohibition, thank God, has a history, and to that we point. Facts settle controversies. We may dispute a proposition, but not a fact. The temperance cause is passing out of the realm of theory, into the assured domain of facts. Through such a transition every cause must pass to victory. Horace Greeley and many other shrewd men ridiculed the idea of an Atlantic cable, and while in the realm of theory no man could say but they had the best of the argument, but when Queen Victoria and President Johnson exchanged congratulations over the newly submerged line, the argument was at an end. The possibility of steam cars drawn upon iron rails was long disputed, distinguished men in the English parliament sustaining its impossibility by strong arguments, but facts have long since performed the offices of the undertaker for these arguments. Theories are the mists of the morning, facts the solid granite of the ages. We are passing out of the period of theories into that of facts in the temperance cause, and only the wilfully blind can now fail to see the value of prohibition. Maine is our color-bearer, and is first entitled to speak in testimony to the practical efficiency of prohibition.

Governor Dingley, in his address to the Legislature in 1874, said:

"This system has had a trial of only twenty-two years; yet its success in this brief period has, on the whole, been so much greater than that of any other plan yet devised, that prohibition may be said to be accepted by a large majority of the people of this State as the proper policy towards drinking-houses and tippling-shops.

"Where our prohibitory laws have been well enforced, few will deny that they have accomplished great good. In more than three-fourths of the State, especially in the rural portions, public sentiment has secured such an enforcement of these laws that there are now in these districts few open bars; and even secret sales are so much reduced that drunkenness in the rural towns is comparatively rare."

Governor Chamberlain, in his message to the Legislature in 1870, said:

"The laws against intoxicating liquors are as well executed and obeyed as the laws against profanity, unchastity and murder."

In 1873, Governor Perham said:

"It is probable that less intoxicating liquors are drunk in Maine than in any other place of equal population in the country—perhaps in the civilized world. Other States have temperance men and women as devoted and as efficient as ours, but, having no laws to aid them, the success they deserve is not attained."

Governor Nelson Dingley, Jr., said, in 1874, to the Commissioners of the Canadian Parliament:

"All organized opposition to the law has died out. The great majority, probably two-thirds of the people at least, heartily approve of it as the best system of restriction of the liquor traffic yet devised, and the most of the minority acquiesce in it as a policy which deserves a thorough trial.

"The great improvement in the drinking habits of the people of this State within thirty or forty years is so evident that no candid man who has observed or investigated the facts can deny it.

"The city of Lewiston (with Auburn), with a population of about 30,000, has not an open dram shop. Secret drinking has not taken the place of open drinking."

Hon. Wm. P. Frye, member of Congress and ex-Attorney-General of Maine, writing to Hon. Neal Dow, says:

"I can and do, from my own personal observation, unhesitatingly affirm that the consumption of intoxicating liquors in Maine is not to-day one-fourth as great as it was twenty years ago; that, in the country portions of the State, the sale and use have almost entirely ceased; that the law of itself, under a vigorous enforcement of its provisions, has created a temperance sentiment which is marvellous, and to which opposition is powerless. In my opinion, our remarkable temperance reform of to-day is the legitimate child of the law."

The above was concurred in by United States Senators Hon. Lot M. Morrill and Hon. Hannibal Hamlin; also by members of Congress J. G. Blaine, John Lynch, John A. Peters and Eugene Hale.

In another letter, addressed to Geo. Shepard Page, Esq., dated Washington, Dec. 22, 1871, Mr. Frye writes:

"The 'Maine Law' has not been a failure in that, 1st, It has made rum selling a crime, so that only the lowest and most debased will now engage in it. 2d, The rum buyer is a participator in a crime, and the large majority of moderate respectable drinkers have become abstainers. 3d, It has gradually created a public sentiment against both selling and drinking. 4th, In all of the country portions of the State, where, twenty years ago, there was a grocery or tavern at every four corners, and within a circuit of two miles unpainted houses, broken windows, neglected farms, poor school-houses, broken hearts and homes, it has banished almost every such grocery and tavern, and introduced peace, plenty, happiness and prosperity. These two things, making the rum traffic disgraceful both to seller and buyer, the renovating and reforming of all the country portion of the State, are the worthy and well-earned trophies of our Maine Liquor Law, and commend it to the prayers and good wishes of all good citizens. . . . Of this law I have been prosecuting attorney for ten years, and cheerfully bear witness to its efficiency whenever and wherever faithfully administered. It has done more good than any law on our statute book, and is still at work. With its provisions you can effectually close every liquor shop outside your cities, and in them make the selling of ardent spirits a very dangerous and risky business. There cannot be found a man in Maine, who is not prejudiced by reason of being a seller, or drinker to excess, or by party passion, who will not concur with me in saying that its blessings have been incalculable, nor a respectable woman who does not pray for its continuance. Thus briefly I have given my testimony, and I know whereof I affirm."

Hon. Woodbury Davis, Judge of the Supreme Court for ten years, said:

"The Maine Law even now is enforced far more than the license laws ever were. In proportion to the number of people participating in the evil to be suppressed, it is enforced in the State as well as are the laws to prevent licentiousness."

Horace Greeley visited the State of Maine in 1855, and in the New York *Tribune* gave the following testimony:

"The pretence that as much liquor is sold now in Maine as in former years is impudently false. We spent three days in travelling through the State without seeing a glass of it, or an individual who appeared to be under its influence, and we were reliably assured that, at the Augusta House, where the Governor and most of the Legislature Board, not only was no liquor to be had, but even the use of tobacco had almost entirely ceased."

All of the prominent pastors in Portland signed the following statement:

"PORTLAND, May 31, 1872.

"As to the effect of the Maine Law upon the traffic in strong drinks, we say, without hesitation, that the trade in intoxicating liquors has been greatly reduced by it.

"In this city, the quantity sold now is but a small fraction of what we remember the sales to have been: and we believe the results are the same, or nearly so, throughout the State. If the trade exists at all here, it is carried on with secrecy and caution, as other unlawful practices are. All our people must agree that the benefits of this state of things are obvious and very great."

Benj. Kingsbury, Jr., Mayor of Portland, and four ex-mayors, united in saying that:

"As to the diminution of the liquor traffic in the State of Maine, and particularly in this city, as the result of the adoption of the policy of prohibition, we have to say that the traffic has fallen off very largely. In relation to that there cannot possibly be any doubt."

J. S. Wheelwright, Mayor of Bangor, says:

"It is safe to say that in our city not one-tenth part as much is sold now as in years past."

A convention of Pastors of Free Baptist Churches in Maine, in 1872, declared:

"That the liquor traffic is very greatly diminished under the repressive power of the Maine Law. It cannot be one tithe of what it was formerly."

J. H. Drummond, formerly Attorney-General, said:

"There were no more violations in proportion to the drinkers, than there were violations of the law against theft in proportion to thieves."

The Hon. Wolcott Hamlin, Supervisor of Internal Revenue for Maine, in 1872, says:

"In the course of my duty as an internal revenue officer, I have become thoroughly acquainted with the state and extent of the liquor traffic in Maine, and I have no hesitation in saying that the beer trade is not more than one per cent. of what I remember it to have been, and the trade in distilled liquors is not more than ten per cent. of what it formerly was. Where liquor is sold at all, it is done secretly, through fear of the law."

Hon. Joshua Nye, late State Constable, and who is as well qualified to speak for the State as any living man, in a letter dated May 18, 1875, gives the following:

"Within the past six months I have visited thirteen of the sixteen counties of Maine, and I know whereof I speak when I say that the cause of temperance never stood so well before. The law is well enforced, and in nearly all the towns no intoxicating liquor is sold contrary to law.

Hon. Neal Dow, in a speech delivered in Association Hall in July, 1875, on the occasion of a reception tendered him by the National Temperance Society on his return from England, said:

"They say the Maine Law has failed even in Maine. Now, Mr. President, ladies and gentlemen, there is not a word of truth in that; it is all false from beginning to end. The Maine Law has not failed, directly and indirectly. Is there not any liquor sold in Maine or in any of the other Maine-Law States? Yes, there is; but you do not infer, therefore, that it is a failure. If you can show that there is as much liquor sold in proportion to the population with the same effect as there was before the Maine Law, that would show the law to be a failure. But in the State of Maine there is not one-tenth part as much of the liquor sold as there was before the Maine

Law. The whole character of the population is changed as the result of that law. There is liquor sold in Maine, but only secretly. I live in the largest town in Maine, and you see no sign of liquor selling anywhere at all. If one went into a hotel and asked for a glass of liquor, I do not know but that a person who knew the ropes might get it. They declare, however, that they honestly keep the law, and apparently they do. Wherever liquor is suspected of being kept with intent to sell in violation of law, the officers search for it and seize it. Every two or three days we have some seizure, but usually in very small quantities—a quart, a gallon, and sometimes only a bottle from the pocket of a man who intends to sell that way.

"I remember the time when there were seven distilleries in Portland, running night and day, at the same time vast quantities of liquor were imported, especially in the ship *Margaret*, one of the most famous ships in New England, whose cargo of St. Croix rum was spread out upon the wharves. How is it now? We have not a distillery running in all the State of Maine, nor is there a puncheon of rum imported. I shall be warranted in saying that there is not one-fiftieth part of the quantity of liquor sold now as was sold previous to the passage of the prohibitory law, but I will say one-tenth. Senators and representatives in Congress, judges of courts, ministers and merchants, have signed certificates which were sent to England, in which they say the quantity of liquor sold is not one-tenth so great as was sold before."

These testimonies ought to suffice to convince any unprejudiced mind. A later statement by ex-Governor Dingley made in a speech delivered in Washington City, D. C., in 1882, is so full as to facts and admirable in spirit as to merit insertion here.

I have been requested to give some account of the practical working of the laws of Maine prohibiting dram shops. I am frequently asked, "Is the Maine Law a success or a failure?" The answer to that question will depend on the standard by which the fruits of the law are measured. If it is asked if the Maine Law has absolutely extinguished secret dram shops, I reply, "No." But if it is asked if it has materially contributed to diminish the dram shop evil, I reply, "Yes." Tested as other laws prohibiting offences against society are tested, and it must be conceded to be a success. No laws—not even the Divine law—do or can extirpate the crimes or wrongs against which they are aimed, although all good statutes restrain and mitigate, so far as it is possible for the law to reach, and thus merit the verdict of success.

It must be remembered that every civilized State treats the liquor traffic not as a legitimate business, to be taken up and carried on by any citizen as a matter of right, as is the case with the trade in ordinary merchandise, but as a source of public danger, which requires the curb of law. Both license and prohibitory laws rest on the assumption that dram shops are an inciting cause of intemperance, with all its gigantic evils, and that their restraint by law can materially strengthen the moral agencies employed to counteract and diminish these evils. Both assume that notwithstanding personal sobriety, as well as other forms of virture, comes from within, and is to be primarily fostered by moral means, yet inebriety, as well as other forms of vice, may come from temptations from without, which it is the duty of the State to remove as far as possible.

The only difference in this respect is in the extent of the protection attempted. License endeavors to prohibit on election days, after midnight, and one day in the week. Prohibition endeavors to prohibit before as well as after midnight, and on every one of the seven days of the week. License prohibits the sale of intoxicants to persons *after* they have become drunkards. Prohibition prohibits the sale to them *before* they are lost, and when the removal of temptation will do good. License assumes that intoxicants sold by legalized dram shops are less harmful than when sold by unlicensed dealers. Prohibition affirms that by licensing dram shops the quality, and even the quantity of the liquors which they sell, remain the same as though they were unlicensed. License assumes that a dram shop having a State certificate of respectability, offers less temptation than one which has no such certificate. Prohibition affirms that the dram shop which the State thus holds up as respectable and safe, is far more dangerous than one which it pronounces illegal and destructive.

Whether the State can more effectually protect her citizens from the temptations of the dram shop by license or prohibitory legislation, may be theoretically debated without other result than to strengthen the disputants on either side. This question, however, must be settled as other questions of public policy ever have been, by the test of experience. What thoughtful men want in matters of public policy, is not so much theory as practice; not so much predictions as performances. We know what is the outcome of the policy of licensing dram shops in this country, for it has been tried for two hundred years, and by every State of the Union. The policy of enforced prohibition, however, has been tried long enough to fairly judge of its influence on the dram shop evil in only two States, and one of those is the State of Maine.

9

A comparison of the results of prohibition in Maine with the results of license in other States, must go far to settle the controversy as to which legislative policy is calculated to afford the better protection against the admitted gigantic evils of the dram shop.

1. It is conceded that prohibition in Maine has practically extinguished the *open* traffic in intoxicating liquors, outside of a very few places, where unfaithful officers are in power; but it is claimed that it has simply substituted the secret groggery for the open and more respectable licensed dram shop, without interfering with the opportunities for gratifying appetite. If nothing more had been accomplished than this, it would be a decided gain to strip from the licensed dram shop the garb of respectability which makes it all the more deceptive and dangerous, and to drive the groggery into corners and holes which respectable men, who have not lost their sense of shame, scorn to enter. The good sense of the Anglo-Saxon mind recognizes the truth that vice outlawed is less dangerous than vice given a certificate of good character by law, and that vicious practices are guaged to a great extent by the opportunities and difficulties of indulgence.

But more than this has been gained. Secret, as well as open dram shops have been extinguished in the rural parts of the State, comprising three-fourths of the population, and the secret traffic confined to the cities and villages. Although this concentration of the liquor traffic in the cities, with the facilities which always exist in crowded populations to evade the officers of the law, has inevitably resulted in less marked progress here than in the rest of the State, yet there is no city in Maine which has as many dram shops, proportionally, as similar cities in license States, while the most of them have far less. According to the reports of the Internal Revenue officers, the average number of retail dealers in the cities of license States, is one to every 175 inhabitants. In only one city of Maine is there found as many as one to 250 inhabitants, while in the cities of Lewiston and Auburn (with a population of 28,000), there is only one to 1,900. All the cities of Maine show an average of one dram shop to every 400 inhabitants—less than half as many as the cities of license States.

It is when we compare the number of dram shops in Maine, as a whole, with the number in other States, that the greater progress made in that State becomes apparent. Fifty years ago, Maine, in common with other States of the Union—all under the license system—had one dram shop to 225 inhabitants. In spite of the counteracting influences of imigration, and of the concentration of population in cities, there has been considerable improvement under the influence of the moral agencies which have been so industriously employed in all the States of the Union, as the latest returns of the Internal Revenue office show now 175,133 retail liquor dealers, or one dram shop to about 300 inhabitants. How much more progress Maine has made, with prohibition as a supplement to the moral agencies everywhere employed, will be seen from the following official returns of the number of inhabitants to each retail liquor dealer in States in different parts of the Union:

State.	One to
Maine	860
Vermont.	600
Massachusetts.	300
Rhode Island.	200
Connecticut.	260

State.	One to
New York	200
New Jersey	200
Pennsylvania	275
Ohio	225
Illinois	300
Indiana	350
Wisconsin	275
Iowa	425
Missouri	350
Louisiana	275
District of Columbia	175
California	100

It will thus be seen that Maine has only one dram shop to every 860 inhabitants—the smallest number of any State in the Union; one-third as many as in Connecticut, Illinois, Massachusetts, Michigan, Pennsylvania and Wisconsin; one-quarter as many as in New York, New Jersey, Maryland, and the District of Columbia and Ohio; and one-eighth as many as California and Colorado; and only one-third as many as the average in the Union. There are three counties, with a population of 100,000, which I have the honor to represent, where there is not a single open dram shop, and in which the vigilant officers of the United States Internal Revenue office have been able to find only fifty secret dealers, or one to 2,000 inhabitants.

2. This advantage of prohibition becomes more striking when we come to compare the sales of secret dram shops of Maine with those of licensed dram shops in other States. It is alleged, for example, that there were last January, 135 secret dram shops in Portland; but the stock in trade and sales of all of them were not as large as one-fourth of their number of licensed places in cities of similiar size. Most of the secret dram shops in Maine

have as their stock in trade a few bottles, or at most gallons of liquor, concealed in some out of the way place, so as to be hastily emptied whenever the officers of the law visit them. In the Editor's Easy Chair of *Harper's Monthly*, George William Curtis, by no means a special friend of prohibition, gave the following account of a personal investigation which he made, as to the manner in which the best secret dram shops are carried on in Maine:

"It is said derisively," remarked Mr. Curtis, "that a man could get as much liquor to drink in Maine as anywhere. And so he might, but not agreeably. The 'Easy Chair' proved it. A vague intimation, consisting of a wink, a smile, and a nod, conveyed the possibility of getting a drink even in the capital city of the temperate commonwealth. Following the wink, like a convict, the turnkey and the 'Easy Chair' passed through the corridors to a door, which was unlocked; then down a narrow staircase into a cellar—and hotel cellars do not always stimulate the imagination; then to another door, which, being duly unlocked and closed, and re-locked upon the inside, revealed a dark, dim room—a cellar in a cellar—with a half-dozen black bottles and some cloudy glass. The cheerful entertainment was at the pleasure of the convict. The turnkey pours out a glass of something and offers it to his companion. It was better than Father Mathew. 'No, thank you; not upon these terms.' The turnkey looked amused. 'Wa'al it isn't exactly gay!' and he swallowed the potion; and leading the way, furtively opened the door again and locked it: and the two revelers, with the jollity of conscious malefactors, stole back again into the light of day.'"

It would take a score of such secret dram shops to do the business and the injury of one gilded licensed open bar. There are twenty licensed places in any of our large license cities, which sell more liquor in one day than all the secret grog shops of Portland last January sold in a week. A gentleman who has good opportunities of knowing the facts, says he is confident that the sales of Maine dram shops are not over $2.00 per inhabitant, against an average of $15.00 per inhabitant in license States.

3. It is frequently charged that there is as much drunkenness—one of the evidences of the extent of liquor drinking—in Maine as in license States; and to support this charge, the arrests for drunkenness in one Maine city are often cited. Comparative statistics of arrests for drunkenness are likely to be misleading, for the value of the comparison depends upon whether the degree of intoxication leading to arrest is the same in the different communities. In Maine it is the practice to arrest every person appearing on the streets under the visible influence of intoxicating liquors. In most other States arrests are made only when the intoxicated persons are quarrelsome, or at least, disorderly.

Again, the concentration of the liquor traffic and the consequent drunkenness of the whole community in the cities and larger villages, makes a comparison of them with the cities of license States, where the traffic and consequent drunkenness are more generally distributed, necessarily inconclusive as to the relative condition of the two. Yet, in spite of this fact, Maine cities show a larger proportion of arrests for drunkenness than similar cities in license States, and their average condition is much better in this respect. The average arrests for drunkenness in all the cities of Maine for 1880, were *twelve* to each thousand inhabitants. The average arrests in sixty license cities from which I have reports, were *twenty* to each thousand. The smallest number of arrests in any license city reported was six to a thousand. The smallest number of arrests in any Maine city was *three* to a thousand. The license manufacturing city of Lowell, Mass., reported thirty arrests for every thousand inhabitants, in addition to a large number assisted home drunk, while the prohibitory manufactoring cities of Lewiston and Auburn, Maine, reported three arrests to every thousand inhabitants.

But when the comparative statistics cover entire States, the number of arrests for drunkenness in Maine is found to be strikingly less than in license States. In three counties of my own district, with a population of nearly 100,000, there were last year only 150 arrests for drunkenness—one and a half to every thousand inhabitants—a number less than one-fourth as large as I have been able to find reported in any license community in the Union.

4. A paragraph has recently gone the rounds, triumphantly asserting that crime—one of the accompaniments of intemperance—has become more frequent in Maine than in license States. The fact is exactly the reverse of this; but the falsehood is still finding willing listeners, while the correction can hardly gain an audience. The false accusation is all the more inexcusable because the State statistics of crime are annually printed and obtainable by everyone who cares to know the truth. I have not time to quote these statistics in detail, but the following table, giving the proportion of convicts of all grades, and the proportion of high

criminals to the whole population of specimen States, will be of interest:

		Convicts.
Maine	1 to	1,600
New Hampshire	1 to	1,260
Massachusetts	1 to	500
Connecticut	1 to	1,000
New York	1 to	690
Indiana	1 to	1,400
New Jersey	1 to	1,000
Maryland	1 to	875
California	1 to	550
		High Criminals.
Maine	1 to	7,540
New Hampshire	1 to	5,500
Massachusetts	1 to	6,000
Connecticut	1 to	3,500
New York	1 to	2,800
Indiana	1 to	4,800
New Jersey	1 to	3,200
Maryland	1 to	3,500
California	1 to	1,000

It will be seen that Maine has a less number of convicts, proportionally, of all classes, and a less number of high criminals, than any State in the Union; 25 per cent. less than New Hampshire, Massachusetts and Indiana; one-half as many as New Jersey and Maryland; and one-third as many as New York and California.

5. There are some results of the temperance movement in Maine, on the basis of moral suasion supplemented by prohibition, which cannot be grasped by statistics, but which, nevertheless, are as tangible and conclusive as a mathematical demonstration. The visitor from a license community, who spends several weeks in this State—not he who simply steams through

in smoking cars and sees mainly hotel life in the cities
—can but be impressed with the fact that drinking
habits are not the rule of our people, but the excep-
tion.   If he sits at hotel tables and participates in public dinners, he will notice the absence of intoxicating
liquors.   If he visits our homes he will find liquors
rarely tendered as an act of hospitality, outside of narrow circles in the city.   If he is present at our elections,
he will see little evidence of their use as a factor in
securing votes, and will observe that candidates for office
prefer to be understood as being either total abstainers
or never more than occasional drinkers.   If he mingles
with crowds on gala days, he will be surprised to notice
how few intoxicated persons are to be seen.

The Canadian Commissioners who visited Maine to
investigate the workings of prohibition, a few years ago,
reported that they attended a State muster where from
10,000 to 15,000 people were present each day for four
days, and yet they did not see half a dozen cases of
intoxication,   At the State Fair in Lewiston, last year,
hardly any drunkenness was seen.   At the 4th of July
Celebration last year at Ft. Fairfield, where a large proportion of the people of Aroostook were gathered, the
newspapers state that there was not a single case of
intoxication.   I have seen more drunkenness on a Saturday afternoon in a Canadian village of 1,500 inhabitants, with two or three licensed groggeries, than I have
observed in a Maine city, ten times as populous in a
whole year.   For this public opinion antagonistic to
drinking habits, we are largely indebted to the educating
influence of prohibition.

These are evidences of exceptional temperance progress in Maine, which demonstrate that the adoption of

prohibition as a supplement to the moral and religious agencies everywhere employed must have greatly aided in mitigating the evils of the dram shop. Indeed, it is observable that those parts of the State in which public opinion has secured the most faithful enforcement of prohibition, are in much better condition in this respect than those places where the enforcement has been fitful and loose; for prohibition, like other laws, can do but little good unless it is enforced; and in this country the measure of enforcement, especially in the case of laws which interfere with greed and appetite, is dependent on the extent and activity of the supporting public sentiment.

The fact that wherever prohibition has been most constantly enforced, there has grown up the deepest conviction of its value, affords the strongest evidence that it has successfully met the final test of all State policies— that of experience. Prohibition was originally adopted in Maine in 1851 as an experiment, which a large number of those who favored its trial regarded as more than doubtful. But the practical test to which it has been subjected, has not only confirmed its friends, but also converted a large portion of its early opponents, until to-day not a third of our people would consent to its repeal.

The beneficial results of prohibition in Maine are too marked to be dismissed with a denial or a sneer. The discussion of the drink problem has passed the stage when it may be turned away with a joke or an indifferent remark, or confined to the sphere of the temperance lecturer and the pulpit. It is more than a question of ethics and moral agencies. It is a question which calls for treatment by the statesman, as well as personal efforts by the philanthropist; which demands the highest wisdom in framers of laws, as well as the earnest efforts of all who mould public sentiment.

In its economic aspects alone, what problem is so serious as this—involving, as it does, a direct annual expenditure, or really waste of more than seven hundred millions of dollars; more than the aggregate of National, State, county and municipal taxation, and an estimated indirect expenditure of as much more in the pecuniary losses and burdens which the accidents, the pauperism, the disease and the crime that flow from the dram shop, impose upon the nation.

In its social and moral aspects what problem is so startling as this? The dram shop is the enemy of the home, which is the basis of individual and national prosperity. It is the foe of health. It is the chief occasion of pauperism. It is the source of a large proportion of crime. It is the efficient ally of vice. It is the prolific cause of untold misery. It is the great obstruction to the progress of Christianity. It is the universal antagonist of good. It intensifies all the perils of our civilization and of our national life. Such a gigantic evil as this calls for the thoughtful consideration and earnest co-operation of every patriot and every friend of virtue and order, in devising and employing the wisest and most efficient measures of restraint and relief.

A very able article appeared in the *North American Review* for 1886, on Prohibition, by D. R. Locke (Petroleum V. Nasby) in which he gives valuable testimony concerning the efficiency of the Maine Law. He says: "Does prohibition prohibit, and is prohibition the cure of the evil? The proof of the pudding is in the eating. I assert that it does, to a sufficient extent to justify the action of the States that have made the experiment, and to encourage those who hope to extend it over all the states. I myself made a tour of Maine, with a view to determining the fact for myself. I explored Portland, the largest city in the State, first. There is liquor sold in Portland, and plenty of it, and yet prohibition has been a pronounced, unequivocal success in that city. Prior to the enactment of the Dow Law, some thirty years ago, there were three hundred grog shops in the city, its population being about 30,000. It was as drunken a city as any in the country, and its rate of poverty, crime and misery was in exact proportion to the number and extent of its liquor shops.

"In 1883, when I visited the city, to determine this question for myself, there were four places only where the law was defied, and liquor sold openly. There were some twenty other places where it was sold secretly, but there were only four open bars, and these four could not be said to be open bars. They were in the sub-cellars under the four principal hotels, and so intricate were the ways to them that a guide was necessary. And when you found them, they were sorry places. A room twelve feet long by six in width, a cold, dismal, desolate room, lighted by one gas light and absolutely without furniture. There was not even a chair to sit upon, only a small bar, behind which were a few bottles of liquors, with the necessary glasses to drink from. Nobody ever penetrated these horrible places except the confirmed drinkers, who must have their poison, and who dare not trust themselves to keep it in their rooms.

"So difficult was it to find, and so dismal and discouraging was it when found, that a Boston man with me remarked: "Well, if this isn't prohibition, it comes very close to it. If I had to take all this trouble to get a drink in Boston, and had no more pleasant place than this to drink in, I don't think I should ever drink."

"This is the strength of prohibition. InPortland there are no delightful places fitted up with expensive furniture, no cut-glass filled with brilliant liquors, no bars of mahogany with silver railings, no great mirrors on the walls, no luxurious seats upon the floor—nothing of the sort. Drunkenness there has no mantle of luxury thrown over it, and the mask of sociality has been ruthlessly torn from it. If you want to get drunk in Portland, you go where the material is, for that purpose, and that only. You must go and find it—it is not trying to find you."

Who have taken the place of these three hundred rum sellers of thirty years ago? Bakers, shoemakers, tailors, milliners, and people of that class. There are no houses vacant, and there is a better class of houses than ever. The effect of prohibition upon the material prosperity of the city is marked. The workingmen own their own houses, their newspapers are better sustained, they have book-stores, art-stores, and all that sort of thing, which a whiskey city of the same population never did sustain; the small trades are all flourishing, and despite the disadvantages the city labors under by reason of climatic and other conditions, it is one of the most prosperous municipalities in the United States. There was once $1,500,000 paid annually for rum—that money now goes into the comforts of life, and there is still a wide margin left for luxuries.

In the county towns of Maine the effect is still more marked. The farmers, when liquor was out of sight,

did not want it, their children grew up without knowing
the taste of the destroyer, and comfort and prosperity
have everywhere taken the place of slovenliness and
unthrift.

The best argument I found in Maine for prohibition
was by an editor of a paper in Portland, who was, for
political reasons, mildly opposed to it. I had a conver-
sation with him which ran something like this:

" Where were you born? "

" In a village about sixty miles from Bangor."

" Do you remember the condition of things in your
village prior to prohibition? "

" Distinctly. There was a vast amount of drunkenness,
and consequent disorder and poverty."

" What was the effect of prohibition."

" It shut up all the rum shops, and practically banished
liquor from the village. It became one of the most quiet
and prosperous places on the globe."

" How long did you live in the village after prohibition? "

" Eleven years, or until I was twenty-one years of
age."

" Then? "

" Then I went to Bangor."

" Do you drink now? "

" I have never tasted a drop of liquor in my life."

" Why? "

" Up to the age of twenty-one I never saw it, and
after that I did not care to take on the habit."

That is all there is in it. If the boys of the country
are not exposed to the infernalism, the men are very
sure not to be. This man and his schoolmates were
saved from rum by the fact that they could not get it till

they were old enough to know better. Thousands upon
thousands of men from other States, who are slaves to the
drink habit, and so securely held by it, that they cannot
of their own power resist, go to Maine that they may
live where it is impossible to procure the stuff which
makes the meat it feeds on. While liquor can be procured anywhere in Maine, if one chooses to go to the
trouble and expense necessary, its procurement is so
hedged about with difficulty that the victim who really
desires to free himself of his appetite generally succeeds.
The help that prohibition gives him is enough to turn
the scale, and he is enabled to let it alone till his restored
stomach and new blood give him will power enough to
do something for himself. It makes a difference with
the man suffering for want of liquor whether he can step
into a bar-room on every corner and take the one drink
for present relief, or whether he has to go to as much
trouble as would pay off a mortgage on a farm to get it.
Hundreds go to Maine for a month or two, and come
back rejoicing in the thought that they are free. That
they do not keep free is owing to the unfortunate fact
that they come back to places where liquor is free, and
they fall.

It is the great trouble with the rum trade that the
producers die off too soon. If a liquor could be invented
that would grip mankind as whiskey does, and at the
same time leave the victim strong to earn money, the
trade would be better. But as the appetite not only
destroys the power of earning money, but cuts the thread
of life very early, new recruits must be made all the
time. It is to the youth of their localities that saloon
keepers look for their victims, and they are as sure to
find them as they are permitted to exist at all.

My editorial friend is a living example of the uses of prohibition. The business of selling rum in his neighborhood was killed when he was a boy, and that saved him. There was no grog seller to hunt him down, and he escaped till he was old enough to know better than to drink at all. Prohibition in Maine saves the youth of Maine.

The experience of Kansas and Iowa has been identical with that of Maine. The prohibitory law is evaded in every possible way. The liquor interest did not at once give up the field, nor has it yet. The saloon was driven out, but its place was taken by secret dives, and by all sorts of devices, some of them very ingenious, to defeat the operation of the law. But the object of prohibition was attained. The gaudy saloon was driven off the streets, the sale of liquor was made illegal and disreputable, and the penalties for violation were made so severe that the seller dare not vend except to those whose confirmed appetites make it entirely safe. The boys are saved. No dealer would dare to sell to a boy, much less to go out and hunt for him. And this is exactly what was aimed at by the makers of the law. The confirmed drunkard will have it anyhow, and it makes very little difference whether he has it or not. The thieves, gamblers and prostitutes will have it, and it makes but little difference how soon liquor wipes them out. But the hunt for boys was at an end. The ghastly mills into whose hoppers were turned boys and girls by the thousands, grinding out daily a doleful grist of prostitutes, thieves, gamblers and paupers, were stopped forever. The law can be and is being evaded to the extent of finishing up the stock on hand, but the supply of new material is cut off. The open saloon is gone, and the coming generation is safe. When the seller dare not sell to boys, the liquor business has a very short life. Nothing is stronger evidence of the success of prohibition in Maine than the devices adopted to evade the law, and continue the sale in a clandestine way. The New York *Independent* gives this as a specimen of such evasions:

"Among the liquor cases in the Supreme Court last year were two where the liquor seized was found under the floor of a water-closet. In another case a barrel of beer was found under a mud-puddle in a yard, a pipe connecting the barrel with a neighboring cellar. In another case the liquor was concealed under a pig-sty. Are we to be told that liquor is sold openly in Portland, when the traffic has been driven into such quarters?"

Having given so much space to the testimony from Maine as the head of the prohibition column it will be needless to go into details in other fields. Human nature is the same everywhere, and the liquor traffic is the same everywhere. When we have a fair example of prohibition before us, as we have in Maine, we know what it is for every other State and country on the earth.

In the year 1880 the state of Kansas, a battle field of ideas, adopted prohibition by about 8,000 majority. For three or four years great efforts were made to convince the public that prohibition in Kansas was a failure. It was declared that its practical effect was to enthrone free whiskey, and to turn the State over completely to the rum demon. Yet, strangly enough, the liquor interest was at the same time employing all its influence for the repeal of the law, only to find that whenever the people had a chance to vote on the subject, the majority for prohibition showed a large increase over that of the previous vote. Its friends became more ardent and more numerous, and its enemies more bitter the longer it was tried, and to-day we might as well attempt to sweep the rich soil of the State into the Missouri River as to wipe out its prohibition sentiment. Kansas is a free State. Free from the curse of human slavery, and free from the greater curse of the rum traffic. We must not close this prohibition class-meeting without giving this bright young State a chance to relate its experience.

"Reports from nearly all the towns and cities in the State are to the effect that the saloon men have quietly closed out the business and have opened up other branches or left the State. As for our own city, we believe that all of the parties heretofore engaged in the business have acted the part of honest, law-abiding citizens, by closing their saloons as far as the spirituous article prohibited by the law is concerned."—*El Dorado Press* (Butler County).

"The misrepresentations of the whiskey men are as miserable in their character as the men who put them in circulation. The report that liquor is sold in this town in open violation of the law is not true. We have also learned from reliable sources that in the great majority of instances the reports of liquor being sold in violation of the law in other towns is equally as false. The men who put these reports in circulation are men who desire to have the law fail, and who hope by the circulation of such reports to break down and intimidate the temperance element. The desire is father to the falsehood. They should remember that the men who fight this question from principle, and not for gain or notoriety, are not the kind of men who are easily discouraged or intimidated, especially by false reports. The law is enforced in this country, and its good effects are apparent upon every hand."—*Independence Tribune* (Montgomery County).

"Does prohibition prohibit? We should say it did, in Parsons, at least. During the month of June last year there were ten arrests for drunkenness. During the two months of May and June there has not been a single arrest. Judge Steel's court has been as quiet as a country graveyard—more quiet, in fact. To make a living the Judge has to file saws, and increase the price of filing. The constables stand on the street corners with nothing to do. Holmes' corner is no longer blockaded with a mass of blear-eyed, bloated bummers, hunting for an invitation to take a drink. Everybody goes about his own business. Everybody is busy. The sound of the trowel and mechanic's hammer is heard in every part of the city. The city is blockaded with materials for new buildings. This is the dull season for trade, but trade was never as good at this time of the year as now. Prohibition prohibits in Parsons, and the people are satisfied with the prospects."—*Parsons Star* (Labette County).

A Winfield brewer says:

"I have invested over ten thousand dollars in my brewery, and I do not believe I could get five hundred dollars for it now on account of the prohibition law. I have ten thousand dollars' worth of beer in my vaults, and am not allowed to sell a drop. My barley and malt cost me ninety-five cents a bushel; but I can't get fifty cents for it now. You have no idea how our people are upset by the new law."

The *Kansas Methodist*, speaking of the State Fair and prohibition, says:

"No thoughtful man who visited the State Fair, or visited Topeka during the week of the State Fair, could fail to observe the beneficent workings of the Prohibition Amendment and Law. The supreme and uninterrupted reign of sobriety, good order, and general good-will and good feeling on the fair grounds, was a practical endorsement that entitles prohibition to the highest premium."

James A. Troutman, Grand Sec. of the Grand Lodge of G. T., and Sec. of the State Temperance Society, says:

"1st. That in a majority of the cities and towns of the State where liquors were previously sold, but little or none are sold now.

"2d. That, with two or three possible exceptions, the traffic has been greatly diminished in all the cities and towns of the State.

"3d. That a large majority of prosecutions have resulted in convictions.

"4th. That in a majority of the counties where the traffic still exists, prosecutions are pending that will ultimately succeed and result in its total demolition.

"5th. That, taking the State over, the sentiment for prohibition is stronger than it has ever been.

"6th. That experience is revealing some defects in our law requiring modification, which the next Legislature will make in the interest of our cause, and which will practically be the last nail in the enemy's coffin.

"7th. That the man who says 'Prohibition is a failure in Kansas,' is a designing enemy, or a misguided friend of our cause."

The Augusta *Republican* says:

"Prohibition may be a failure, but since the law went into effect last May there are about five hundred calabooses in the towns of Kansas standing empty."

The Prohibitory law was amended one year ago, and it is being enforced as well and with as satisfactory results as its most sanguine friends could expect.

Governor John A. Martin, in his annual message, January, 1886, said:

"The general working of the amended prohibitory law of last winter has been favorable. Organized opposition to the law is fast disappearing, and the general and popular feeling is positively and decidedly in favor of obedience to the Constitution as amended. Not only the Supreme Court, but all the judges of the District Courts of the State and the judge of the United States Court for this Circuit, are in favor of allowing the people of Kansas to regulate their own domestic affairs in their own way. Thus all agencies have worked together, during the year, in behalf of law, order and practical temperance, and Kansas has made a greater moral progress than in any other twelve months in her eventful and noble history. On the 1st of January, 1885, saloons were open in twenty or thirty towns and cities of the State. A year later the open saloons had been banished from every town and city of Kansas, with possibly two exceptions, and in these active and determined legal efforts for its suppression have been instituted.

" I firmly believe this happy consummation is approaching a realization. Steadily and surely intemperance is decreasing in Kansas, drinking habits are giving place to sobriety, and public sentiment is deepening and strengthening in favor of wholesome and practical laws to extirpate the open saloon and the vice, the crime, the poverty, the suffering, and the sorrow of which it is the fruitful source."

Under date of April 12, 1886, J. A. Troutman, Secretary of the State Temperance Union, and thoroughly posted in all these matters, says:

"There is not a paper in the State of general circulation and State influence opposing us. The three great dailies which gave us lots of trouble are now with us— the Atchison *Champion*, Topeka *Commonwealth*, and the Leavenworth *Times*. The only place in the State where saloons run regularly is Leavenworth. They have been closed as tight as a drum in Atchison. In Dodge City and two or three other places they are spasmodic."

The last State Convention of the State Temperance Union unanimously adopted the following:

"After nearly five years of trial, we find the following results of the operation of the law:

"The wholesale liquor trade within the State has almost ceased.

"The sale of liquor as a beverage has been immensely diminished.

"The open dram shop is almost entirely gone.

"The secret places in which liquor is sold in violation of law have been greatly reduced in number, and the general sobriety and wonderful prosperity of our people are matters of universal comment by strangers who come within our gates."

Hon. S. B. Bradford, Attorney-General of the State, says:

"Kansas has a population of about 1,250,000 people; it has eighty-five organized counties; in sixty-two of these counties only 525 convictions have been had for the violation of the various criminal laws of the State since January 1, 1885; that 235 of that number are convictions for the violation of the prohibitory law. Fifty-two of the eighty-five counties in the State report that they have no saloons. Eight of the other counties report that the law is only partially enforced.

"From all the information I have been able to obtain, it appears to me that the prohibitory law is no longer an experiment, but, on the contrary, is being enforced as successfully as the law against horse-stealing, murder, arson, or other crimes known to our statute."

The Toledo *Blade* sent a special representative to Kansas, who made a careful investigation, and says:

"In summing up the result of my investigations in Kansas I do not hesitate to say that, taking everything in consideration, prohibition is a success. Of the two thousand and more cities and towns that I visited, but two ran the rumholes in full blast—Atchison and Leavenworth. At Wichita and Dodge City I found that the law was less strictly enforced than it should be, while the nearest approach to perfection existed in Topeka, Lawrence, Ottawa, Emporia, Arkansas City and Newton. In the small towns and in the country the vast majority of the people are prohibitionists, and are thoroughly with the law as it now stands. A few malcontents can be found who want to be classed with the 'I told you sos' if the law should be repealed, but as that event is not likely to come about in a year or two at most, their ranks are likely to be thinned out very materially before their day of jubilee comes around.

"I am satisfied that, aside from the two cities that I have mentioned, not an open saloon exists in the State.

"Over two-thirds of the saloons have been closed, the cases of drunkenness have been reduced one-half, saloon keepers have been made to feel that the business is not a profitable one within the borders of the State, and the popular seal of condemnation has been placed so emphat-

ically upon the whiskey business that the habitués of
the saloon and the old topers are, in many instances, shut
off entirely from temptation, and are compelled to keep
sober for want of something to make them drunk."

GOVERNMENT PERMITS.

James A. Troutman, Esq., Secretary of the State Temperance Union, in his last annual report, referring to the
tax receipts of the Internal Revenue Department, which
is so often referred to as "evidence" against prohibition,
says:

"One of the sources of annoyance to prohibitionists is
the constant reference by whiskey men to the number
of Government permits issued to liquor dealers in the
State. I have had so many letters from outside of the
State, asking for the facts, that I thought it not inappro-
priate to explain the matter in this report.

"That the number of permits issued in this State is
large, is certainly true. A moment's reflection, however,
will show that the number of permits issued is not even
prima facie evidence that the same number of saloons or
drinking places exist. In the first place, every druggist
in the State, whether holding a probate judge's permit
or not, must have a Government permit. There are in
round numbers 1,500 druggists in Kansas, which accounts for the equal number of Government permits. I
have in mind now a saloon keeper who took out a permit and opened a saloon, but was soon compelled to close
up. He moved to a neighboring town, and repeated the
experiment, with the same result. He went to a third
town, and for the third time within a year attempted to
run a saloon, and failed. At each place a permit was
taken out. Then there are instances where the proprie-

tor and two or three clerks hold permits to retail liquors
at the same place. This, of course, is done to enable
them to change proprietors frequently, for the purpose
of defeating prosecutions. If A is prosecuted, he claims
that B is the proprietor. If B is the victim, he claims
that C is the proprietor. Government permits are essential in such an emergency to keep them out of the
clutches of Uncle Sam, for whom the average saloon
keeper has a profound reverence.

"The saloon and dive takes a permit, runs a few days,
and is compelled to close up. The saloon or drinking
place is gone, but the record of the permit remains in
the collector's office during the whole year. A permit
issued to a dealer who runs a clandestine dive only
twenty-four hours makes as big a showing against us—
to those who do not understand it—as though he had
run 365 days in the year. The great number of permits
issued, instead of indicating a great number of saloons in
Kansas, is rather indicative of the fact that for the past
year saloon keepers have been 'kept on the jump.'"

Governor Martin a few weeks ago bore the following
testimony to the success of the prohibitory law:

"During the past eleven weeks I have been through
all parts of the State, speaking at fairs and reunions once
or twice every week. These gatherings have numbered
from two to six thousand people. My opportunities for
finding out the true status of the enforcement of the prohibitory law have been unequalled. During this time I
have been struck with the entire absence of drunkenness.
In fact, incredible as it may appear, I did not see a
drunken man through my whole circuit. Here in
Topeka, at the reunion, the largest gathering ever held
in the State, where no less than one hundred thousand

people were present, only one case of intoxication came under my observation. It is my opinion that not more than one-tenth of the liquor is sold in the State to-day that there was before the passage of the prohibitory law."

The Baptists of Topeka have sent a greeting to their fellow-members throughout the country, in which they affirm the success of prohibition in Kansas. They say:

"Not a legalized place for the sale of liquor as a beverage in all our eighty thousand square miles of territory. In four years we have driven the saloons out of nearly three hundred towns and cities of the State. We have seventy-five counties without a saloon, and for this token of Divine favor we return gratitude to Almighty God. There are but three cities in our State that openly violate the law. Two of them are on the banks of the Missouri River, the other near the Colorado line, all on the border of States unfriendly to the prohibition laws; but at these places the State and county officials have commenced prosecutions, and they will soon have to submit to the inevitable."

These testimonies might be continued at great length, but those already offered are sufficient to convince any unprejudiced mind of the success of prohibition in Kansas. The expected improvements in the law alluded to in some of the testimonies here given, have been enacted by the Legislature, and recent convictions obtained that indicate the absolute destruction of the open saloon in the State. One violater of the law, against whom complaint was made on several counts, has just been sentenced to pay a heavy fine and to eighteen years imprisonment. Such sentences as that will not long leave the question in doubt whether or no prohibition is a success in Kansas. It is not prohibition but the liquor business that is a failure in Kansas, and that is why the liquor dealers are so anxious to convince the country that prohibition is a failure.

Iowa was the the next State taken by the irresistible battallions of our prohibition army. The enemy was fully aroused by the crushing defeat suffered in Kansas, and employed all its forces in contesting this field. Contributions of money, sympathy and encouragement were sent from all parts of the land to the liquor forces, and they contended as men fight for their lives. A more hotly contested field has never been known in the history of the reform, for it would presage general defeat 'to lose two such states as Kansas and Iowa in so short a time. But valor, intimidation, the free flowing barrel and bribery were all in vain, for when the votes came to be counted in June, 1884, it was found that a large majority had been cast for prohibition. Every means was employed to override the law, and finally a technical defect in the method of its adoption was discovered, and the law declared null and void. Then it was declared in a jubilant way that there had been a great reaction in the public mind on the subject, and that the next vote would show a heavy vote against prohibition. This prophecy had in it about the same element of Divine inspiration that characterizes the voluminous predictions of the liquor party. Inspired it undoubtedly was, but by a lying spirit sent forth to deceive, for the second vote and all the subsequent votes on the question in the Legislature have given increasing majorities in favor of prohibition and its enforcement. The testimony as to the practical working of prohibition in this State is of the same nature as that already given from Maine and Kansas, and, therefore, need not be here reproduced at great length. In that state Governor Sherman, in his retiring message, January, 1886, said:

"Singularly enough, the law for the suppression of of the liquor traffic has had to contend, not only against a vigorous onslaught of its enemies, but as well the apologies of its hypocritical friends, whose cowardly acts have really been more deadly in character. And yet, struggling with all these elements, the law has sustained itself. I am persuaded that there is less of liquor drinking in Iowa than previously; less of crime which grows out of the sale and use of liquor; and, therefore, the law has been a source of public and private good. All this stimulates its better enforcement. After quite a thorough and patient investigation, I am satisfied that the law is very generally observed throughout the State, and has more of the intelligent public endorsement than when enacted two years ago. It must be continued, therefore, and as far as possible made more vigorous."

Over fifty editors, representing fifty of the leading newspapers of Iowa, recently signed the following document:

"The undersigned, members of the Iowa Press Excursion to the Pacific Coast, have found one report here which is unjust to the State which we love and honor. It is that the statute incorporated in its laws prohibiting the common sale of intoxicating liquors as beverages is not and cannot be executed. Representing different parts of the State, we testify that the prohibitory statute, considering the short time since it was enacted, is as well enforced throughout the State generally as other laws, and it is daily growing stronger in public sentiment, and will become the permanent policy of the State. We ask the attention of the press of the Pacific Coast to this correction of erroneous and unfair statements."

Hector Ballendon, writing from Burlington, April 7, 1886, to the N. Y. *Evangelist*, says:

"Not in the history of our city has such a blessed state of affairs reigned as at present. A walk up and down our streets fails to reveal a single open saloon. No attempt on the part of the saloon keeper at conceal-ment is made. Curtains are rolled up, screens rolled away, and through the open glass nothing meets the eye but empty tables and counters, or in some instances the placard 'For Rent.' Only to-day two drinking men told me it was next to impossible to get a drink, one having spent part of a day in the company of a stranger (strongly desirous of 'wetting his whistle') in the vain pursuit. Across the street from my office are two of the largest, oldest and wealthiest saloons. One was closed by law; the other took alarm, and closed up voluntarily. Old frequenters passed by with a thirsty countenance and sad shake of the head. The uninitiated rush up, seize the latch, which does not yield, and with a sur-prised look walk away. In weeks I have seen but one drunken man. Of the sixty or seventy of these places, which marred the beauty of our city, and destroyed its peace and happiness, not one, even in the outskirts, is to be found open!"

The Toledo *Blade's* special representative, deputed to make a careful investigation of the practical results of prohibition in Iowa, says:

"Over two-thirds of the saloons have been closed, the cases of drunkenness have been reduced one-half, saloon keepers have been made to feel that the business is not a profitable one within the borders of the State, and the popular seal of condemnation has been placed so emphatically upon the whiskey business that the habitués of the saloon and the old topers are, in many instances, shut off entirely from temptation, and are compelled to keep sober for want of something to make them drunk."

Rev. M. Bumford, of Fairfield, referring to the enforcement of the prohibitory law, says:

"So far as can be learned, about five-sixths of all the saloons and liquor houses in the State have been closed up. Probably eight-ninths of the population of the State have no open saloon or other drinking place within easy reach. There are no open saloons, in fact, except in some of the larger cities, such as Burlington, Davenport, Dubuque, and Council Bluffs; and very many of the saloons even in these places are closed. Prosecutions are being brought against those which are open. Liquors are, no doubt, still sold secretly in many places, and will be, most likely, for a while, though the vigilance of the Law and Order Leagues will gradually hunt them out."

H. L. Chaffee, of Des Moines, Iowa, in the *Northwestern Christian Advocate*, writes:

"We are frequently asked by our Illinois friend, whether 'prohibition prohibits.' Yes, it does prohibit, and is just as well enforced in the city of Des Moines to-day as any criminal law. Do not infer from this that we are lax in the enforcement of all law, for such is not the case. Hardly a city in the West of this size is as peaceful and orderly. One year ago we had sixty saloons in full blast, each paying $1,000 a year license. To-day we have not an open saloon."

Bishop Bowman, of the M. E. Church, says:

"During the last six months I have had good opportunity to see the work of prohibition in Iowa and Kansas, and to gather the facts in regard to it from those having ample means to know all about it. It gives me great pleasure to say that in those States prohibition does prohibit. I have seen no drinking, and well-informed persons have assured me that the traffic has almost ceased in the larger portions of those States."

Senator Clark introduced a bill into the Legislature, providing for additional penalties, which was adopted and approved April 5, 1886. It is known as the "Clark Combination Lock," and is one of the most severe laws in its penalties ever passed. The following is a synopsis of the law:

"Actions to enjoin nuisances under the prohibition law shall be brought in the name of the State by the district or county attorney of the proper county. In case he refused, any citizen of the county may do so. The general reputation of the place shall be admissible as evidence. The court in session, or the judge in vacation, shall grant a temporary injunction without bond. Whoever is convicted of keeping a nuisance under the prohibition law shall be fined not more than $1,000 nor less than $300, and the party shall not have an opportunity to purge himself. If the existence of the nuisance be established it shall be abated under the judgment of the court by seizing and removing all movable property within the building, and by securely closing the same, if the property of the defendant is not used as a homestead, for one year unless sooner released as provided. The owner may secure the opening of the building by filing a bond to the value of the property, and giving satisfactory evidence that the nuisance shall be abated. In all prosecutions under the State prohibition laws, the finding of

such liquors in possession of any one not legally authorized to sell the same, or in a private dwelling, shall be
presumptive evidence that the same were kept for illegal
sale. Second conviction punishable by a term of not less
than three months nor more than three years in the penitentiary. Any person or company illegally transport-
ing prohibited liquors, upon conviction shall be fined
$100 for each offence, and committed to jail until such
fine is paid. A refusal to correctly brand or make known
contents of any package, or falsely mark the same with
intention to conceal contents, shall be fined $100 and
costs. Peace officers shall have power to break open and
examine any packages. The property, except homestead, of any person convicted under the provisions of
this act shall be confiscated to pay fine and costs."

The following section shows the "grip" of the law :

"SEC. 1558. For all fines and costs assessed, or
judgments rendered, of any kind, against any person for
any violation of the provisions of this chapter, or costs
paid by the county on account of such violations, the
personal and real property, except the homestead and
the personal property of such person, which is exempt
from execution, as well as the premises and property,
personal or real, occupied and used for the purpose,
with the knowledge of the owner thereof or his agent,
by the person manufacturing or selling or keeping, with
intent to sell intoxicating liquors contrary to law, shall
be liable; and all such fines, costs and judgments shall
be a lien on such real estate until paid. And where any
person is required by Section Fifteen Hundred and
Twenty-eight (1528) and Fifteen Hundred and Twenty-
nine (1529) of this chapter to give bond with sureties,
the principal and sureties on such bond shall be jointly

and severally liable for all civil damages, costs and judgments that may be adjudged against the principal in any civil action authorized to be brought against him for any violation of the provisions of this chapter, costs paid by any county for the prosecution or on account of any violation of the law prohibiting the illegal sale of intoxicating liquors, that would be a lien on the property under the foregoing provisions and including costs paid in seizure and condemnation proceedings, may be covered by such county, by the enforcement of such lien by execution, or by action against the owner to subject the property to sale for the payment thereof. And evidence of the general reputation of the place shall be admissible on the question of knowledge and written notice given him or his agent by any citizen of the county shall be sufficient to charge the owner with knowledge under the provisions of this section."

The reports show that in the large towns and cities where the traffic lingered for lack of enforcement, the saloons are fast passing out of existence.

The *State Register* of Des Moines says:

"The Clark bill is doing the business for the saloons. Twenty of them closed business in Des Moines last Saturday, as many more have closed the present week, and all are making ready to go. Up and down Walnut and Locust streets big placards 'For Rent' voice the surrender of the saloons to the new law. Some of them are being made over for the occupation of legitimate business, others will soon be torn down to be replaced by new brick blocks, and the general line of their rapid retreat is seen on every hand. Ever since the Clark bill passed the Senate they have been packing their traps and making ready to go."

11

Again says the *Register*:

"'The Clark Combination Lock,' as the saloon keepers have named the new act for the better enforcement of the prohibitory law, is not only rapidly and peacefully closing the saloons in the interior cities and towns but also in the river cities as well. It seems to supply 'a long-felt want'—a demand for legal and automatic methods for enforcing an important law. Even in Burlington it has closed one hundred and thirteen saloons."

The Dubuque *Prohibitionist* says:

"Several saloons have just been closed at Iowa City by perpetual injunction. Also the two breweries. . . .

"All the saloons in Waterloo are closed; in McGregor they are quitting the business, and in Cedar Rapids thirty have already announced their intention of obeying the law. At Ottumwa several violators are in jail."

The Executive Committee of the State Temperance Alliance issued an address April 15, 1886, in which they said:

"Another year of the conflict has now passed, and with great pleasure, and profound gratitude we are enabled to congratulate you upon prohibition assured. Instead of repealing the prohibitory law, as predicted and demanded by the saloon power, the General Assembly has given us the additional prohibitory legislation necessary to close all saloons in the State.

"Prior to the recent session of the Legislature the Alliance appointed a committee to prepare and secure the enactment of a bill embodying the amendments necessary to make the law more easy of enforcement and effective. That action resulted in the production of the bill introduced by Senator Clark, called the 'Clark

Bill,' which was passed with some slight amendments, and constitutes chapter 66 of the acts of the Twenty-first General Assembly. The experience of the last two years had suggested the needed changes, so that by this act the law is so amended as to make it impossible to successfully run a saloon where there is an earnest desire on the part of any citizen to prevent it. This act was passed by an increased majority over that for the law two years ago. This indicates the increasing strength of prohibition, and continued healthy condition of public sentiment on this subject which is highly gratifying. Its passage has had a marked effect already. Hundreds of saloons throughout the State have voluntarily closed within the last few days. In Des Moines and other cities and towns local organizations and private citizens have done a noble work in enforcing the law as it was, and the saloon keepers were becoming discouraged, and as soon as the ' Clark Bill ' passed they began to quit of their own accord. Of all the places in Des Moines where liquors were unlawfully sold there are now only eight places open. The keepers of these deny selling, and diligent search and inquiry has failed to discover evidence of violation of the law. So that we may safely claim that the saloons are practically closed in the Capital City. The saloon power seems to be utterly discouraged, and about to yield the contest, but we warn the friends against the fatal error of trusting the law to enforce itself, or being lulled into false security by our wily and unscrupulous adversary. There is too much gain in the iniquitous business to admit of easy suppression, but this law, as amended, gives the friends of prohibition the power to effectually suppress it. Let us use the weapons now placed in our hands; attack this great enemy of the homes and human happiness wherever he appears. The decree has gone forth, 'the saloons must go.' 'Let them not stand on the order of their going, but go at once.' Make the contest 'short, sharp and decisive.' Drive every saloon keeper out of the business or out of the State, and Iowa shall be wholly redeemed from the curse of the traffic."

The Burlington *Tribune*, a liquor paper, says:

"Since the Clark bill has become a law, 113 business places in Burlington have been closed as far as we have been able to learn this morning. They were saloons and places where intoxicating liquors were sold. But the closing of this kind of business places is not the only consequence of this infamous law. Other branches of business are affected thereby, for instance, cigar manufacturers, butchers, bakers, manufacturers of soda water and ginger ale, and who knows how many more, not to mention the brewers and manufacturers of wine. The owners of houses, too, will soon realize that Burlington is only a 'Deserted Village,' as described by Goldsmith."

The following despatches are published in the Des Moines *Register:*

"WATERLOO, April 13.—All the saloons in the city were closed to-day by order of the mayor, in accordance with the Clark liquor law, and quiet reigned. The proprietors state that they have closed for good. Reports from adjoining towns show the same state of affairs."

"MACEDONIA, April 13.—The law-abiding citizens of this place rejoice to see crape tied to the door of the only saloon in this town. We have formed a Law and Order League, which means the enforcement of law."

"SHELDON, April 16.—The grand new county of

O'Brien can now boast of not having a saloon or semblance of one within its handsome borders. Six weeks ago there were twelve of these pests in the county running in full blast."

"OSKALOOSA, April 16.—The saloon men of our city all, save one, have gracefully thrown up the sponge and yielded to the inevitable, 'thus saith the law.' There may have been one, but the writer has not seen an intoxicated man on our streets for a week."

"SIGOURNEY, April 20.—No open saloons now in Sigourney. One man is laying out a sentence in jail under the old law. Our saloons have thrown up the sponge, and some of them will move to Nebraska and start in business. The last grand jury brought in sixty indictments, and the most of them were for selling liquors. Prohibition will prohibit. Let the good work go on."

"WHAT CHEER, April 20.—This city has been rated one of the worst inland towns in the State for an open defiance of prohibitory liquor laws. But twenty-three saloons now wear on the front doors, 'Clark's Combination Lock,' and the business men who formerly took any interest, are now organized to enforce the law, should they re-open. Peace reigns supreme."

From all parts of the State there are cheering reports of the decrease of crime and pauperism. The Des Moines *Register* for May 1st, 1887, publishes from advance sheets of the Secretary of State's Annual Report, some remarkable facts that exceed the most sanguine expectations of the prohibitionists. The figures are official and reliable. The report gives the names of fifty-five counties that for one year have not had a single occupant of their jails. Fifty-five of the ninety-nine counties have no saloons and empty jails. What state, where prohibition does not exist, can present such a record? Iowa, no less than Kansas and Maine, gives an unqualified, enthusiastic testimony in favor of prohibition. Before the facts here given by competent witnesses, all theories about the difficulty of enforcing, and the demoralization of the public by failure, are as chaff before the wind.

But prohibition has not been limited to northern States. It has been established in a large number of southern counties and cities, though as yet no State has adopted it. Under a local option law, which is to many a very acceptable form of prohibition, allowing the people to determine for themselves in each voting precinct, whether liquor shall be sold or not in their precinct. Large portions of Maryland, Florida, Tennessee, Alabama and Georgia, are enjoying the blessings of practical prohibition. No where has there been a more vigorous contest, with a free use of all the tactics so common and effective in the hands of the liquor dealers, than in Atlanta, the metropolis of Georgia. Financial interests, and the pride which the citizens justly feel for their beautiful city, were appealed to in the assertion that the success of prohibition would ruin the business of the place, leave half the buildings without occupants, turn trade to other less fanatical cities, and strike as with a death paralysis the wonderful prosperity of that most enterprising of southern cities, and furthermore, that the southern people would never submit to its enforcement if adopted. In spite of these objections, urged with great persistency by some of the best citizens, the intelligence, courage and conscience of Atlanta were equal to the occasion, and prohibition was adopted, though by a small majority. The Atlanta *Constitution*, in June, 1887, gives a very clear statement of the results of prohibition in an experience of a year and a half. We here re-produce it as an unanswerable response to all croaking about failure. It is an appeal to matter of fact, whatever anyone may think or fear; this declares what actually is. Many prohibitionists feared for the results in Atlanta because of the small majority, the bold pretentions of the liquor interest, and the nearness of anti-prohibition communities where liquor could be bought and smuggled into the city. But the testimony of all classes has dispelled these fears, but no one has stated the case better than the *Constitution:*

"The election at which prohibition was put on trial in this city is entitled to a place among great events. No election of a local nature was ever before held in a city of sixty thousand people in which more was involved. The changes proposed by it were so radical as to be almost revolutionary. Over a hundred business houses were to be closed. Nearly five hundred men were to be forced to give up a chosen employment. The city treasury was to be left with forty thousand dollars less revenue. Trade amounting annually to millions was to be turned away from the city. Many large business houses were to be left unrented. Of course, a movement proposing measures so radical met with the most spirited and determined opposition. Many of our best citizens regarded it with outspoken disfavor.

" It was said that prohibition in a city so large as this was impracticable, that it would not prohibit, that the trade would be injured, that taxes would be increased, that the stores in which the liquor business was carried on would not be rented for other purposes, that the same amount of whiskey would be drank with the law as without it, the city would only miss the revenue, that it would be a death-blow to Atlanta's progress.

"It has now been eighteen months since the election, and twelve months since the law went into effect. We are prepared thus from observation to note results.

"Prohibition in this city does prohibit. The law is observed as well as the law against carrying concealed weapons, gambling, theft and other offences of like character. If there had been as many people in favor of carrying concealed weapons, theft, gambling, etc., as there were in favor of the retail of ardent spirits, twelve months ago, law against these things would not have been carried out as well as it was against the liquor trade. In consideration of the small majority with which prohibition was carried, and the large number of people who were opposed to seeing it prohibit, the law has been marvellously well observed.

"Prohibition has not injured the city financially. According to the assessors' books, property in the city has increased over two millions of dollars. Taxes have not been increased. Two streets in the city, Decatur and Peters, were known as liquor streets. It was hardly considered proper for a lady to walk these streets without an escort. Now they are just as orderly as any in the city. Property on them has advanced from 10 to 25 per cent. The loss of forty thousand dollars revenue, consequent on closing the saloons, has tended in no degree to impede the city's progress in any direction. Large appropriations have been made to the Water Works, the public schools, the Piedmont Fair, and other improvements. The business men have raised $400,000 to build the Atlanta and Hawkinsville Railroad. The number of city banks is to be increased to five. The coming of four new railroads has been settled during the year. Fifteen new stores, containing house-furnishing goods, have been started since prohibition went into effect. These are doing well. More furniture has been sold to mechanics and laboring men in the last twelve months than in any twelve months during the history of this city. The manufacturing establishments of the city have received new life. A glass factory has been built. A cotton seed oil mill is being built worth $125,000. All improvement companies, with a basis in real estate, have seen their stock doubled in value since the election on prohibition.

"Stores in which the liquor trade was conducted are not vacant, but are now occupied by other lines of trade. According to the real estate men, more laborers and men of limited means are buying lots than ever before. Rents are more promptly paid than formerly. More houses are rented by the same number of families than heretofore. Before prohibition, sometimes as many as three families would live in one house. The heads of those families now not spending their money for drink, are each able to rent a house, thus using three instead of one. Working men who formerly spent a great part of their money for liquor, now spend it in food and clothes for their families. The retail grocery men sell more goods and collect their bills better than ever before. Thus they are able to settle more promptly with the wholesale men.

"The perceptible increase has been noticed in the number of people who ride on the street cars. According to coal dealers, many people bought coal and stored it away last winter who had never been known to do so before. Others who had been accustomed to buying two or three tons on time, this last winter bought seven or eight and paid cash for it. A leading proprietor of a millinery store said that he had sold more hats and bonnets to laboring men for their wives and daughters, than before in the history of his business. Contractors say their men do better work, and on Saturday evenings, when they receive their week's wages, spend the same for flour, hams, dry goods, or other necessary things for their families. Thus they are in better spirits, have more hope, and are not inclined to strike and growl about higher wages.

"Attendance upon the public schools has increased. The Superintendent of Public Instruction said in his report to the Board of Education, made January 1st, 1887:

"'During the past year it has become a subject of remark by teachers in the schools and by visitors, that the children were more tidy, were better dressed, were better shod, and presented a neater appearance than ever before. Less trouble has been experienced in having parents purchase books required by the rules, few children have been withdrawn to aid in supporting the family, the higher classes in the grammar schools have been fuller, and more children have been promoted to the high schools, both male and female, than ever before in the history of the schools. All these indications point to the increased prosperity of the city, and to the growing interests in the cause of education on the part of the people.'

"There has been a marked increase in attendance upon the Sunday-schools of the city. This is especially noticeable among the suburban churches. Many children have started to the Sunday-schools who were not able to attend for want of proper clothing. Attendance upon the different churches is far better. From fifteen hundred to two thousand people have joined the various churches of the city during the year.

"The determination on the part of the people to prohibit the liquor traffic, has stimulated a disposition to do away with other evils. The laws against gambling are rigidly enforced. A considerable stock of gamblers' tools, gathered together by the police for several years past, was recently used for the purpose of making a large bonfire on one of the unoccupied squares of the city. The city council has refused longer to grant license to bucket shops, thus putting the seal of its condemnation upon the trade in future of all kinds.

"All these reforms have had a decided tendency to diminish crime. Two weeks were necessary formerly to get through with the criminal docket. During the present year it was closed out in two days. The chain gang is almost left with nothing but the chains and the balls. The gang part would not be large enough to work the public roads of the county were it not augmented by fresh supplies from the surrounding counties. The city government is in the hands of our best citizens.

"The majority in this county in favor of prohibition was only 235. Such a change has taken place in public sentiment, however, that now there is hardly a respectable anti-prohibitionist in the city who favors a return to bar-rooms. There are some who would prefer high license, or its sale by the gallon, but it is a remarkable fact that there is no disposition to have the saloon opened again. The bar-room has gone from Atlanta forever, and the people with remarkable unanimity say amen! There is very little drinking in the city. There has been forty per cent. falling off in the number of arrests, notwithstanding there has been a rigid interpretation of the law under which arrests are made. Formerly, if a man was sober enough to walk home he was not molested. Now, if there is the slightest variation from that state in which the center of gravity falls in a line inside the base, the party is made to answer for such variation at the station house.

"Our experience has demonstrated to us beyond a doubt that a city of sixty thousand inhabitants can get along and advance at a solid and constant rate without the liquor traffic."

The same testimony in substance comes from all parts of the State of Georgia, where prohibition has been tried. Senator Colquitt, with as clear an eye and as honest a heart as any man in the South, paused in the press of official duties to give the following word of good cheer to the friends of this cause:

"United States Senate, Washington, D. C.,
March 30, 1886.

"Prof. W. W. Smith, Ashland, Va.:

"*Dear Sir:* A very few words will do for an answer to your letter of inquiry as to the effect on taxation, and property values in Georgia as the result of prohibition. The allegation that these have been affected injuriously is simply a device of the enemy. There has not been the fraction of a mill added to our tax in Georgia by reason of prohibition, nor, taking values in Atlanta as an index, has there been any falling off in real estate prices. In my State, as everywhere else, business is halting and dejected; but will any zealot for whiskey and whiskey civilization and prosperity say that the one million of workingmen now out of employment in the

United States are thus placed because of the stoppage or reduction of their whiskey ration? I think it is high time for men to take up their slate pencils and figure out what 'a boom' in dollars and cents is worth to any people that has to be secured by the degradation and ruin of a large proportion of the population who contribute the 'blood money' that enters into the bank balances. In the estimation of some of our latter-day economists the redemption of immortal souls from brutish enslavement to strong drink is entirely too dear if it is secured by a sinking in trade quotations or an inconvenient hindrance to the downward plunge to perdition, temporal and eternal, by closing the corner groggery. This is the stupid logic of sin,'defiant, hardened and desperately selfish. We must give up such public spirit and political economy as this, or stand by and see our christian civilization, thwarted and disgraced.

A. H. Colquitt."

Rev. Dr. A. G. Haygood, of Emory College, Oxford, Ga., says:

"There is not an informed man in Georgia who does not know that the prohibition counties have enforced prohibition—to say the least that can be said—as vigorously as they have enforced other laws. More—during the Atlanta campaign abundant testimony from county officers was brought forward to show that more convictions were obtained before the courts for illicit selling in prohibition counties than for any other violation of law. This statement illustrates the wisdom of the local option effort: the county that gave a good majority for the law had the moral force to enforce it.

"It is true that some liquor is 'smuggled' into the dry counties; just as some foreign goods are smuggled into our ports. The Philistine press makes the most of every such case ; but their sneers do not deceive men who know the truth of things. It stands to reason that the licensed, well-advertised bar-room sells more liquor than any underground, outlawed concern can sell. For example, I saw, last summer, on a car leaving a 'wet town,' a negro man carrying an old corn-sack to a 'dry town.' He said that he had several bottles of whiskey in the sack ; it was evident that he had a quantity in him. It was at night, just before day. He had been sent down early in the night, to return late in the night, with liquor for the Sunday drinking of parties in the dry town. Does any man in his senses believe that this method of securing Sunday drink sells as much liquor as did the eight or ten bar-rooms in that town sold before prohibition—rigid enough to compel the employment of the colored brother and his corn-sack—was adopted?"

Rev. Dr. J. B. Hawthorne, of Atlanta, in a letter written March 29, 1886, says :

"The liquor dealers and their servile dependents tell you that prohibition is a failure in Georgia, when the records of the criminal courts show that in every county which has adopted it, crime has been reduced not less than 90 per cent. They tell you that it has greatly impaired the value of real estate in Atlanta, though the assessed value of her real estate is a million and a half dollars greater than it was a year ago. They tell you that it has killed the business of Atlanta, when it is an admitted fact that, in comparison with other cities of the South, the present activity in business circles is almost phenomenal. They tell you that business men are leaving us. The doggery keepers, drunkards, gamblers, loafers, dead beats and prostitutes are leaving—just these and no more.

"Atlanta is prosperous and happy. Her virtue-loving people have risen up in their majesty and stamped out what they felt to be a curse and disgrace to their community, and their homes and hearts are full of sunshine and gladness."

The Grand Jury of Cobb County Superior Court for November term, 1885, said :

"It is a subject for profound congratulation that, since the adoption of prohibition, crime has wonderfully decreased, the moral atmosphere has been purified, and peace and good order prevail. Quiet reigns where once scenes of disorder and confusion were supreme. Property values have increased ; our towns show unmistakable evidences of prosperity, and our people universally endorse the change."

The Savannah *News*, one of the largest and ablest of the daily papers in the South, in a recent editorial said :

"More than three-fourths of the counties of the State have voted out whiskey, and there is not one of them that is not richer and more prosperous for its action. In every one of them the people are happier and more industrious, and there is less crime and pauperism than there ever was before. The prohibition movement in the State has grown rapidly, because wherever it has been adopted its benefts have at once become apparent."

The Alabama *Prohibitionist* says :

"Labor has improved 100 per cent. in the counties in Georgia where prohibition has been adopted. The business men are fast becoming prohibitionists, as a matter of business, and now wonder why they could not see before that the money spent in saloons belongs to those doing legitimate business, and giving value received in

return for cash. Men are now saving money, and looking forward to the day when they shall own houses and
lands for themselves.

The following telegram is from La Grange Co.:

"Before prohibition we had thirteen bar-rooms. The
antis said it would ruin our town, but since its adoption
about $150,000 have been permanently invested; twenty
new houses now going up, no vacant stores or residences,
and our town greatly improved. Our people unanimous
as to good done by it morally and financially."

Similar testimony might be given from Maryland,
Texas, Arkansas, Kentucky, Tennessee, Pennsylvania,
Vermont and Rhode Island, but this reiteration of sub-
stantially the same facts from different localities is in
danger of becoming monotonous, and with abundant
material unused we here bring it to a close. This testimony is an appeal to matter of fact, the process by
which all sound reasoners wish to arrive at their conclu-
sions. In directness, volume, variety, fullness, force,
breadth of scope, and eminence of the source from which
it is derived, it must seem to every unprejudiced mind
conclusive. The question whether prohibition will prohibit, is clearly answered by this overwhelming array of
evidence.

But it is said that these successes among agricultural
people, in thinly settled States, and in counties far
removed from the great centers of population, prove
nothing for the nation at large, for the manufacturing
and the mining districts and for the great cities. It may
be freely confessed that prohibition has not yet been
attempted in the fields where its execution would be
attended with the greatest difficulties. But let us
remember that but a little while ago our opponents were

just as confident that prohibition could not be enforced
in these communities where it has won such splendid
and complete success, as they now are that it cannot be
made effectual in the large cities. As they were mistaken
in the one case, it is reasonable to suppose they may be
in the other.

Experience proves that prohibition is like a descending
avalanche, the farther it goes the greater its force. Prohibition helps prohibition. Its success in one community prepares the minds of the people for it in another.
Atlanta was possible because Maine, Kansas and Iowa
had gone before. As the area of prohibition enlarges,
the public mind will adapt itself to it. Friends and foes
will come to understand and adjust themselves to its
force. Already it has, by its successes, invaded the
daily press and modified its tone toward temperance
work. Its force has been felt in legislative halls, and in
many of the States not yet ready for prohibition, more
restrictive measures have been adopted. The public
mind is being educated to expect a decisive movement
against the common enemy of God and humanity. If it
may be granted that a prohibitory law could not now be
enforced in New York, Philadelphia or Chicago, it must
be granted that its enforcement is now possible in many
places where five years ago it was not possible, and that
if the present rate of growth in public sentiment continues for the next five years, it will be possible to enforce
it even in these large cities, the strongholds of the rum
traffic as of every iniquity. In the city of Philadelphia
for instance, there has been, through the act of the last
Legislature, a much heavier license fee levied on the
saloons. It is estimated that this higher fee will close
one-third of the saloons. If the next Legislature shall

12

still further increase the tax and reduce the number, the evil will be diminished, the public mind educated to the idea of the amenability of the traffic to law, and the saloon keepers themselves have a forewarning of the inevitable doom awaiting them, and for which they will have to prepare themselves as best they can. With actual prohibition spreading into new localities where the sentiment is most favorable to it, and by its fruits creating a sentiment that will welcome it in still other communities, and by the ever tightening restrictions which this enlarging area of prohibition sentiment must place upon the traffic in its strongholds, the enemy will at last be so reduced in resources and broken in spirit that the citadels of his power can be carried by storm without serious difficulty. I do not concede that prohibition in these large cities is certainly impossible at the present time, but if anyone insists that it is, the above outline seems to suggest a plan of campaign, the natural method of growth by which in the near future it will be not only possible but an actual reality.

No great reform has ever been more successful than prohibition so far as tried. But if not a complete success, is that a sufficient argument against it? It is the office of law to educate the people by setting before them correct rules of living, by which they may form their lives according to noble and pure ideals. It is the devil's own proposition to debase the rules of living till they harmonize with the corrupt lives of those to whom they are to apply, through the fear of demoralization, because of the pernicious influence of an example of law-breaking. If the law is debased, by what rule, or what foundation, and from what ideals will you project a reformation? Let the law be pure and good, though all men be sinners. It is said that "a prohibitory law would be promotive of a law-breaking spirit, for a community learning to break one law, will speedily learn to break all laws." How unfortunate that such wisdom should be confined to the liquor interest. The ten commandments must be responsible for a large share of the world's wickedness if this principle be true. What a dismal failure they have been for three thousand years. They have been trampled on with impunity, and yet it does not seem to have occurred to Jehovah to withdraw them to avoid the demoralization of a law-breaking spirit. Why does he not give the people a law that they will keep, and thus avoid the terrible demoralization of law-breaking? Since people will steal, and a law prohibiting it will be a failure, would it not be better to be on the winning side, and make stealing lawful under certain regulations, that the people would not be compelled to debauch their consciences by breaking the law in order to steal? The law does not prevent murder, therefore would it not be better to strike the much to be desired harmony between law and practice, by legalizing murder and stopping this law-breaking spirit, by which people are learning to disregard law? The seventh commandment may be wise and good in itself, but it is constantly violated, it is a failure, and the public is demoralized by this example of law-breaking, therefore would it not be better for the morals of the community to do away with the law, and put an end to marriage ceremonies and vows? Is not heaven in fact plotting the ruin of this world by setting up a law so high and pure that it is constantly violated, and mankind demoralized as a consequence? Isn't it time that the wisdom developed by the experience of the liquor dealers was in some way communicated to the Supreme Ruler, the monstrous folly of the prohibition of all iniquity pointed out, and the better way of saving men by giving them a law that they will obey, pressed upon the attention of the Supreme Intelligence? Does this not look business like? The decalogue has been a failure, the death of Christ was a failure, Christianity is a failure, Christian preaching has been a failure, but we must have success. Therefore let us abandon all these impracticable and demoralizing methods and theories and adopt those that will be successful, and thus by giving the people a law that they will obey, we shall make their salvation easy. Do we need to follow this logic further? Does not everyone see that it is the old gospel incident repeated again? The devil from a high mountain points out "all the kingdoms of the world," a wide universal success, and "says you ought to have this, it is for you, you can obtain it, fall down and worship me, and all shall be yours." Demoralization of the people by a law they cannot keep, is the devil's criticism on the Bible from beginning to end. Our friends, however, need not fear the demoralization of the people through the failure of a prohibitory law, for as we have shown, and as they well understand, it is not the law, but the liquor business that will prove a failure under prohibition.

CHAPTER XII.

POLITICS.

THE proposition advocated in these pages, that the liquor traffic be prohibited by law, looks toward legislation and so falls within the domain of politics. It is not strange that to many, its entrance into politics seems like a shell thrown in from the camp of the enemy, liable to explode any moment, and from which it is best for all parties to keep at a safe distance. It is not the kind of a new comer those who manage affairs like to see entering the political arena. It is not sufficiently accommodating, does not respect sufficiently old party tactics, makes too much of conscience and the public good, is not facile enough in making and entering into compromises to secure party success, is too independent and resolute about its own measures, and altogether, is such an one as politicians must regard with misgivings.

It is said to be a disturbing element in politics. If it would really become this it might prove to be the greatest blessing of the age. Certainly nothing is more needed than that some such angel should come down from heaven to trouble the waters of "the muddy pool of politics," that some of our maimed, halt, blind and palsied politicians might step in and be healed, and so be able, successfully, to run the race in which they have hitherto been beaten. The politicians, however, seem as much frightened as were the timid, storm-tossed disciples when they saw Christ walking toward them on the water, but if they would only receive this prohibition angel into their ship the storm would cease, and "immediately" they would be at their desired haven.

A disturbing element in politics, that is, some new ideas and principles, something expressing and enlisting the conscience of the people, calling forth their deepest and purest convictions, bringing into active prominence their noblest impulses and deepest thoughts, something that will open a thousand pure fountains of religious thought and feeling into this stagnant "pool," is the greatest need of the times, and the one hope for a purer political condition. Demoralization in politics quickly follows intellectual stagnation. Indeed, they interact one upon the other, and where both exist politics soon sinks to a mere trade, a dexterous handling of forces to secure certain results. When great moral questions are brought to the front, the leaders of discussion take a lofty position, and are stimulated to the highest exercise of their abilities, while the people respond to an appeal made to their consciences by a more generous exercise of that faculty in all the affairs of life. Many unjustly fear great controversies, and apprehend dire results from heated debates, but if the question be of a moral nature and the appeal to conscience, the hotter the debate and the keener the birth pangs, the grander the moral revolution about to be ushered in. Demosthenes thundering against the moral lethargy of Greece, Cicero unmasking the hideous form of treason, Patrick Henry standing on the shores of the new world to advocate the cause of human liberty, Daniel Webster pleading for national unity and fraternity, Charles Sumner advocating the rights of four millions of oppressed and despised human beings, and Wendel Phillips entreating his countrymen to free themselves from the great curse of strong drink, are sufficient illustrations of how ability and genius rise to their sublimest heights by adhering to great moral subjects. Great heroes are born of great conflicts. Great minds are developed in dealing with great subjects and leading great enterprises. In the midst of the agitation which attends the process of great moral reforms, the worst elements are often thrown to the surface, giving the superficial observer the impression of great demoralization, but in fact it is only the process of throwing off these base qualities. In the moral as in the natural world stagnation is corruption and death, agitation, purity and life.

It does not require great acumen to see that the past twenty years have not been years of great living ideas in the political world. There have been no great moral questions, for which men have been willing to suffer and to fight in the name of right, of humanity, and of God. Questions touching the moral life of the nation and of the individual have been crowded out of political discussion, or treated to a few high-sounding platitudes that might be interpreted to suit the varying sentiments of voters in different communities. Great questions have knocked at the door, questions suited to the brain of a Clay or a Webster, but our politicians have been so busy looking after party interests, that they have been politely dismissed with a request to call at a more convenient season. We have scarcely had the strength to be frank, and certainly have not been sincere, true and courageous with the poor Chinaman, who, like a pale moon, has hung in the western sky of our political horizon. A

vast amount of indifferent rhetoric has been expended on
the pestilential Mormon, but instead of solid shot aimed
at the heart of the evil, with a view to putting an end
to it, our politicians have contented themselves with
throwing rockets into the sky over Salt Lake City, for
the amusement and entertainment of their constituents.
There has been no little discussion about the elevation
of our vast population of Negroes, but the chief question
with politicians has been as to who should have the
benefit of their votes. On the one side, there has been
a great clamor, and a good degree of courage, in insist-
ing upon a free vote and a fair count, so long as it was
probable that the votes would be in the interest of that
side. On the other, there has been no disposition to use
shot-guns or other impediments so soon as it became
apparent that it was to be favored by the votes cast.
The greatest question of all, the temperance question,
great in all the elements that appeal to the calculating
brain, the feeling heart, and the guiding conscience, has
not even been treated to the doubtful compliment of an
ambiguous allusion, till a rude blow on the cheek from
its honest right hand roused the slumbering genius of
the political caucus. We have been living on the ideas
of a former generation, fighting over its battles, burying
its dead, canonizing its saints, and from sheer moral
apathy and intellectual languor, refusing to fight the
greater battles of to-day, formulate new ideas that would
shine in the sky of the world's progress for a thousand
years, and develop saintly, heroic characters that would
inspire and bless the toilers for God and humanity till
the latest generation. Campaigns have been conducted
by the discussion of subjects made popular by the heroic
devotion which other men brought to them in lives of

suffering, and which they forever settled by going into the grave in their behalf, while the sublime themes of these pregnant times had not a tongue to give them voice. When the contest has seemed doubtful, our astute statesmen have resorted to the shrewd expedient of tearing open the graves of our fallen heroes and displaying before deeply moved audiences the clothing pierced by musket shot or saber thrust, that upon these awakened sensibilities and rekindled animosities they might engraft the claims of their candidate, while not an allusion was made to the men falling every day in our streets by the hand of a cruel foe, who every year slays more men than ever fell in battle in a single year on this continent. Sectional feelings have been revived, the passions of war have been rekindled, and old animosities have been resurrected, while the precepts of the Prince of Peace, good will to men, and healing for the nation, have been persistently put aside. According to our own political teachers, our principles are in the history of the past, our heroes in their graves, and our saints in heaven. It is a decaying age that employs its talents in building the tombs of the prophets of the past.

In our politics, the supreme effort has been to secure and hold the offices. Two tasks have been set before the politician as necessary to success. The first was to secure a commanding position in his party, the second, to secure the supremacy of his party. To fail in either was, according to the faith of the times, to merit political damnation. This has brought to the front the organizer of partisan forces, the manipulator of the caucus and the convention. Statesmen were neither understood nor appreciated, principles were out of date and were remanded to the fanatics, conscience was made for church and sunday-school, here but one thing is paramount, and that is party ascendency.

All this time great questions have been waiting for some one with heart and brain large enough to take them in, and be lifted to greatness by them in reflecting their light upon the minds of the people. If disposed to confine his view to the financial aspect of the subject, what a magnificent field does the temperance cause open to a man with the genius of a Pitt? Was there ever a greater opportunity for a man of real power? Or if he were to consider the social and physical well-being, what an incomparable opportunity is afforded for the versatile eloquence of a Clay! If he would denounce with burning eloquence oppression and wrong to the weak and helpless, and plead with words of flame for outraged women and dishonored children, how much superior the temperance theme to that which made Patrick Henry and his words immortal! It seems to be proof of intel-lectual as well as moral decay in the realm of politics, that such great themes waiting about us, and appealing to us by all the considerations that have most power with men, shall fail to enlist the talents of our aspiring statesmen.

It is not remarkable that with the exclusion of great moral questions from politics, the whole matter of state-craft should degenerate into a dexterous manipulation of forces with a view to the partisan control of the offices to be filled, and that the more gifted and conscientious of our citizens should turn to other fields for worthy occupation. Naturally, also, would follow what men of all parties bewail, but none seem to have power to cor-rect the wide-spread demoralization of the suffrage by the unblushing use of money in the purchase of votes. A man who would feel that he was profaning sacred things by selling his vote where a great moral question was pending, might have no such feeling, and might regard his vote as a proper article of merchandise, where only a choice between two parties or two men was to be determined. The sacred right of suffrage ought always to be held as a thing far above the purchasing power of money, but it is very natural when citizens see their trusted leaders excluding from politics the great moral living questions of the time, and devoting themselves to the work of securing party ascendency for the control of office and financial profits that belong to them, to catch the infection and consider the whole business a matter of traffic and trade, of barter and sale. With a selfish, mercenary, or partisan object set before the people, it is idle to expect high moral character in political action, a deep sense of the sacredness of the suffrage, or a lively interest in preserving to all the right to cast an unconstrained vote. With a low aim, we shall have low methods and low practices. Bribery at elections, the sale of votes to the highest bidder, is the natural sequence of the perversion of the functions of government from the Divine idea of the good of the people to a partisan or personal end. If conscience and high moral purposes do not rule the leaders in party action, it is idle to expect them to rule their supporters at the polls. If those who formulate the political faith of the people sell the sacred interests of truth for popular favor and the emoluments of office, the citizen will imitate their example by selling his vote. We shall never have a pure suffrage, free from bribery and constraint, till we set before the people a political object that will appeal to conscience, patriotism and intelligence. While our aims are partisan, selfish and corrupt, we set before the people the example and offer the most powerful persuasion to corruption in political action. You can neither convince a man of the sinfulness of selling his vote, nor of the duty of protecting others from violent constraint, or a dishonest count of their votes, so long as the objects set before the people, for which they are to vote, wear the aspect of a bargain for the purpose of evading great moral questions that involve the most sacred and important interests of the ·people. To purify and protect the ballot, we must elevate the whole plane of political action, recognize and maintain the sacredness and high moral character of political duties, make our appeal to conscience and the sense of right in man, then will we have a basis on which to make our claim and an example by which to enforce it.

Just such a question as is necessary for political reformation is presented in the cause of temperance. Aside from the great good to be accomplished in the suppression of the liquor traffic, the moral elevation of politics by the introduction of such a question, would, in itself, justify the most earnest efforts in its behalf. Whatever we may think of the propriety of making it a political question, it is now too late to consider that matter, for prohibition is already in the field with a cordial reception from the people that indicates that it is quite welcome to stay as long as it pleases. What the friends of this measure ask is that the leaders in political action shall take notice of it and give the people an opportunity to express themselves concerning it. The second thing we ask is that the people will rise above party or personal fealty in devotion to principle by voting for this measure wherever it is possible. It ought not to be regarded as asking too much that conscientious, intelligent men would rise above party on a great question like this. Bondage to party is as base and as contrary to true freedom as bondage to a monarch or a task master. He is not free who is not at liberty to obey his conscience and his judgment as to what is right. Nothing can be more painful or discouraging to the true patriot than to see godly men, who pray in church for righteousness and peace in all the earth, go into the street and vote at party dictation for the continuance of the liquor traffic. The safety of the republic and the perpetuity of our free institutions demand a race of intelligent freemen over whose head no party leader dare crack his whip; men who can neither be bought nor sold, flattered nor intimidated, men who have principles for which they are willing to suffer, and which they hold above party allegiance, and for which, if necessary, they are willing to cross party lines. The question of the form of political action in the interests of the temperance cause is one upon which all friends of the cause do not think alike. Many intelligent, earnest advocates of prohibition have thought that a separate political party in its interest the wisest form of action. I have requested the Rev. George K. Morris, D. D., a very earnest and able advocate of this view, to give a brief statement of the grounds upon which the Prohibition party rests its claims to public support. In response he kindly furnishes the following:

"1. The two great parties are out of date. They are a political anachronism. Their lines were drawn on issues that are now ancient history. Hence the classification of votes which was effective during war times has come to be ridiculously unserviceable for conditions so greatly changed. Men who favor prohibition, the great question of the hour, divided on questions of minor importance, go gravely to the polls and cast votes that cancel each other, leaving liquor men in command of the situation politically.

"The temperance issue must be forced. The friends of strong drink must, as a strategic measure, be driven into one party, and compelled to do openly, before all the world, what they now do, and long have done, adroitly, secretly and hypocritically, that is make their business their politics. This will drive all good men to the other side, where, voting together, they will make short work of the bad business. Then the traffic in intoxicants will not only be forbidden by law, but actually annihilated as a business, by a great and vigilant party created for that very purpose.

"2. The old parties do not aim at prohibition. That, they say, is impossible. The utmost they promise is restriction, and that coupled with permission, legalization, protection. Even this 'half loaf, with poison in it,' is promised only under pressure from the new party, because the leaders have discovered that 'something must be done to hold the temperance vote.'

"3. The old parties cannot be trusted. Even when they want to be honest they cannot. The facts forbid. They need the votes both of temperance and whiskey men. To hold both they must deceive one or the other interest. As a rule they choose to deceive prohibitionists. Notoriously their record is one of broken promises. It is folly to trust them longer. They dare not keep their word.

"It has been so easy to blind temperance men to the

real situation that they have long been the laughing
stock of the adroit men who so shrewdly emasculate
them politically. Politicians habitually say 'we must
do something for the liquor men, or lose their vote:
temperance men can be trusted not to leave the old
party.' And it is true. The new party aims to change
this matter.

"4. The new party has proved itself the best possible
agitating agent. Before its birth the press generally
ignored the temperance movement. Now the papers are
full of it. Its present standing before the public could
not have been gained in another half century of purely
non-partisan effort, judging from the past.

"This is the natural result of organization, the effect of
forces left inert by every other method.

"5. History proves that temperance laws, however
mild, do not enforce themselves, and that officers of the
old parties dare not enforce them, because of the votes
enforcement would cost. The most effective assertion
against prohibitory laws, is that, 'prohibition does not
prohibit.' This has been said so after that the unthink-
ing among all classes believe it true. And yet it has
absolutely no foundation save in the fact that no honest
attempt is made to enforce temperance laws. Law and
order societies are a standing indictment of the govern-
ing parties. They strive to do, at private expense, what
is treacherously left undone by those who were elected,
and are paid by the public to do. Hence the necessity
for a party to enact and honestly enforce its own law.
Prohibition on any other basis will not be worth having.

"6. It is certain that the temperance vote can never be
unified, concentrated for prohibition, except by the new

party. Temperance men in the Democratic party will never leave their party to elevate the Republican party to power, nor will Republicans generally ever vote for a Democrat because he is a temperance man. But an enlightened conscience will surely lead good men from the old parties north and south to forget old animosities, and unite for God and humanity under the unstained banner of the Prohibition party. The victory that can be won thus, and only thus, will repay all it costs."

In some of the states the friends of temperance have combined under a pledge to vote only for men known to be favorable to their cause. Thus the whole temperance vote was carried in a body from one party to the other, according to the character of their nominations, and where the existence of such a pledge was known before-hand it had a marked effect upon nominations, for there would be a very earnest desire to win this vote. It has been comparatively easy in this way to secure legislation such as the friends of the cause desire. It does not seem to lay a heavy requirement upon the Christian voter, to ask him with men of his own and of the opposing party to stand together on this principle and to give their united strength to the party candidate, who will pledge himself, if elected, to support their cause, and it affords the prospect of immediate success without a long, bitter partisan struggle.

Still others hold absolute non-partisan action to be the wiser course, as it is with murder, theft and other crimes. They hold that public sentiment and not party rules this country, and that public sentiment is often stronger without a party in its support. They point with pride to the fact that wherever prohibition has been adopted it has been on this plan, and that all partisan

efforts have been failures. Prohibition has won its vic-
tories by having a day set apart for the vote on this
question alone, with no candidates to be elected and no
other questions to complicate the measure, so that people
from all parties could unite in this measure without
deserting their own political organizations.

They regard the tenure of party supremacy as very
insecure. It is probably for the public good that it
should be so, and they are, therefore, unwilling to commit
the sacred cause of prohibition to the inevitable vicis-
situdes of party life. They prefer to lodge their cause
in the public conscience, rather than commit it to the
tricks of politicians, the fate of an unpopular candidate
or the overthrow of some political revolution. No party
can long hold power, there always must be alternation
between parties, but prohibition must be perpetual and
universal, and, therefore, it dare not rest upon any party
organization.

They also claim that non-partisan action is the only
form by which a prohibitory law can be enforced. The
triumphant enforcement of the laws in the states that
have adopted prohibition, indicated by the howls of the
liquor dealers and the shouts of the friends of temperance, is abundant proof that prohibition can be enforced
on this plan. It is alleged that it could not be enforced
on a partisan basis for this reason: every prosecution
would partake of the nature of a political contest,
because its success or failure would strengthen one party
and weaken the other, and thus all our party machinery
and tactics would be carried into the courts, which
would utterly break down all just administration. It is
now very difficult to convict and punish men for crimes
which are by all men acknowledged to be crimes, but if

a powerful opposing political party was interested to bring all its influence and machinery to bear upon the pending cases, and if it was supported in its efforts by the presumption that the prosecution was undertaken for political purposes to strengthen the opposite party in its hold upon the offices and positions it held, a reasonable expectation of justice from the courts would be at an end. The strength of justice in the courts is that its claims are pressed in the interests of morality, of the public good, and of eternal righteousness, and not of any man's political aspirations, or of any party's claim to political ascendency.

All these lines of effort, no doubt, are marching toward the one great result which all desire, and when they converge to a given point, if not before, prohibition will be triumphantly established.

It is too late to talk of keeping the question out of politics. Whatever we might wish about it, the issue is already made in the political field, and no one can be indifferent to the results, for they will exercise a potent influence upon the interests of society and of the individual as well. If we had declined to make it a political question, our opponents would have thrust the issue upon us, for they have boldly entered the political arena with such tactics as are in harmony with the business they represent. Mr. D. R. Locke, with peculiar opportunities for learning the facts upon this point, gives the following testimony concerning it: "In party contest this power has two points to make. First, to demonstrate that it is a power which is not to be meddled with. No matter whether the candidate aims at the Presidency, a seat in Congress, some collectorship, or a park commissionership, the first question the Liquor Dealers' Association asks, is, 'Is he a temperance man?' If he is, the whole power of the organization is turned against him. They want it understood that no one can be elected to any place of honor or profit without their help. The showing of this power insures them against such troublesome inter-ference as the enactment of early-closing laws, Sunday closing, large taxation, and above all, prohibition. They aim at control of the law-making power as well as the law-executing power. Secondly, they want their places to be made the centre of political management, the places where committees meet, and from whence money used in the election is to be dispensed. From this money they take their toll, as a matter of course. The point with the brewer is to make the brewery the one controlling element in politics, and he has succeeded wonderfully. A politician may safely snub the Church, but he grovels in the dust before the wielder of the beer-mallet. He pays no attention to the good classes, but how he bows to the worst! The reason is, the good classes are divided on political and economic questions, while the liquor interest is united solely for one end.

Once more, as to their strength: add to this vote (which is, of itself, enough to turn the scale as parties are now organized), the collateral branches of trade more or less connected with liquor making and selling. The tobacconists, the coopers, the bottlers, and the different kinds of people who supply the saloon trade, are all under this influence, and half as many more can be added to this 1,600, making it 2,400.

But this, large as it is, is the least of it. There is not one of these eight hundred saloons that cannot control four votes besides the two behind the bar, and that comes very close to a full half of all the votes in the city.

They control the poor devils who are glad to sell their
votes for the beer they can drink, a week or two before
an election, and one day after.

Now take this enormous vote, mass the men employed
in breweries, the wholesalers and retailers of liquor, the
bartenders and other assistants directly employed, the
collateral branches of trade dependent more or less upon
them, and the vast army of hangers-on of the saloons,
and it is a power which can and does control the cities
of the country. Parties vie with each other in bidding
for the saloon vote, nominations are made with sole reference to it, and this unholy power would become the
government but for the counteracting influence in the
country, which is yet to some extent free from its infernal influence. Think of a government under control of
an organization whose business it is to make criminals
and paupers. Think of a government controlled by the
worst, instead of the best citizens. Think of communities
governed by the men whose business it is make thieves
and paupers, instead of honest and self-supporting citizens. The influence of rum in politics is one of the
strongest reasons for prohibition. Since the liquor traffic
has so boldly entered the political field, the friends of
temperance have no choice left about meeting them in
that field unless they basely surrender to be ruled by it.

The importance of harmony of action also becomes
apparent in presence of this united, compact, mighty
force. It has been the weakness of our cause that the
friends of temperance have not agreed as to method, and
often more force has been employed in combating some
department of the temperance army than in efforts to
subdue the common foe. Such things grieve and dis-
courage good men, and give great joy in the camp of the

enemy. Nothing pleases the arch foe of human happiness better than divisions and conflicts between the various temperance factions, and if he can in any way aid and embitter these divisions he would gladly pour out his money for such a purpose. It is, perhaps, too soon to expect absolute harmony of method, but is it too soon to expect harmony of spirit? Are the men engaged in this great moral reformation so small and narrow, so uncharitable and bitter, so coarse and violent as to indulge in suspicion, accrimony, abuse and denunciation of their fellow workers who choose different lines of effort? Is it not possible to do the work of Christ in His Spirit? Must we degrade ourselves in order to lift up others? Is it necessary to show the worst tempers and attributes of the human mind in the effort to suppress vile passions? Does not intemperance of speech and conduct in our efforts to suppress intemperance in strong drink react against our fundamental principle? Is not he the worst enemy of our cause who, attaching himself to one line of effort, employs his strength in denouncing the methods, impugning the motives, and denying the sincerity of those who choose to work in other ways? The apostles' rule is a good one for temperance workers as well as others: "Let all bitterness, and wrath, and anger, and clamor, and evil speaking be put away from you, with all malice; and be ye kind one to another, tender hearted, forgiving one another, even as God for Christ's sake hath forgiven you." We have great need here to cultivate that charity that "thinketh no evil," that "beareth all things, believeth all things, hopeth all things." Anyone who rises to the sublimity of true temperance work, will have cordial encouragement for, and a hand to help, all who fight against the common foe.

CHAPTER XIII.

OUR FORCES.

THE temperance sentiment, which for a hundred
years has been growing in this country, has taken
a variety of organic forms. There are those who think
it would be more effective if not divided into so many
distinct lines of effort. These different organizations
sometimes come into collision, divert attention from the
common foe, bring reproach upon the cause, and create
bitterness and opposition where love and co-operation
ought to exist. Their existence gives ample proof of
the wide extent and vigorous character of the temperance sentiment out of which they arise. Great tidal
waves of excitement have swept over the country at
various times, always, like the inundations of the Nile,
leaving the common soil fertilized and enriched for the
growth of an intelligent sentiment on this subject. It
is well to look over this past, study its great epochs, cel-
ebrate its achievements, learn wisdom from its defeats,
and gather inspiration from the lives of its grand heroes.
For more than a hundred years, with the great awakening of Christendom to a more earnest religious life, the
temperance reformation has been advancing. Often it
has met with defeat and suffered reaction, but the tide
soon changed and came thundering in with a volume
and force greater than before, showing that the great
ocean of humanity was back of it, and was moving for
its support.

One of the first definite appearances of this great revolution was a remarkable publication in 1785, by Dr. Benjamin Rush, of Philadelphia, under the title, "*A Medical Inquiry into the Effects of Ardent Spirits upon the Body and Mind*." This is an ably written, clear and bold argument for total abstinence. He maintains that the habitual use of distilled liquors is useless, pernicious, and universally dangerous, and that their use as a beverage ought to be wholly abandoned. Dr. Rush was a man of exalted character, of great learning, one of the signers of the " Declaration of American Independence," and his book produced a profound impression, and seemed to give body and voice to the rising sentiment of the young republic on this subject. There had been other significant expressions on the subject, but none crystalizing the best thought of the times as did this book. A few years before this, a volume of sermons appeared, which also were attributed to Dr. Rush; in which the evils of intemperance were pointed out in strong terms. This book had the effect of inducing the physicians of the City of Philadelphia to unite in a memorial to Congress, in which they compare " the ravages of distilled spirits upon life " to those of " plague or pestilence," only " more certain and extensive," and pray Congress to " impose such heavy duties upon all distilled spirits as shall be effectual to restrain their intemperate use." A like course in these days might be set down to the credit of wild fanaticism, for there would certainly be little ground for supposing that Congress would take any notice of such a petition. These memorialists, however, had some warrant for their action, for in 1777 Congress actually adopted the following resolution on the subject: " Resolved, that it be recommended to the several legislatures of the United States immediately to pass laws the most effective for putting an immediate stop to the pernicious practice of distilling grain, by which the most extensive evils are likely to be derived, if not quickly prevented." Other steps were taken in those early days, showing that this great reform was even then on its way, but there is general agreement in dating its historical life from the publication by Dr. Rush in 1785. This publication, which was subsequently enlarged and published in many editions, was not all that Dr. Rush did for the cause. By addresses on important occasions, and by articles issued through the press, he stirred the public mind on this subject.

Another prominent figure in these early days of the reform was that mighty preacher and great agitator, Dr. Lyman Beecher. About the time of Dr. Beecher's appearance as an advocate of the cause (1808), the first temperance organization was formed in Saratoga County, New York. Rev. Dr. Herman Humphries also became an advocate of the advancing movement, and many others of less fame aided the good work.

In 1813 the Massachusetts Society for the Suppression of Intemperance was formed in Boston, the object of which was "to suppress the too free use of ardent spirits, and its kindred vices." Dr. Eliphalot Nott, President of Union College, greatly aided the cause by publishing a volume of sermons about this time on the evils of intemperance, and many of the best minds of the period gave it their cordial support.

In 1826, under the leadership of Dr. Edwards, a few friends of the reform organized in the City of Boston the American Temperance Society. In April of the same year, Rev. William Collier established in Boston the first newspaper devoted to the cause, under the name of *The National Philanthropist*.

The reform was now making rapid progress, and in 1832 Gen. Carr, the Secretary of War, abolished the spirit ration in the army, and issued an order prohibiting the sale of distilled liquors by sutlers. Up to this time the war had been waged against distilled liquors only, as the evils of intemperance were chiefly confined to the use of these.

It now appeared, however, that many drinkers signed the pledge of abstinence from distilled liquors, but continued to be drunkards by the use of other drinks. Mr. Luther Jackson, of New York City, prepared a pledge of abstinence from all intoxicating drinks, and secured many signers. To him belongs the honor of inaugurating this new era in the history of the reform. In May, 1833, the first National Temperance Convention was held in the City of Philadelphia, at which there were four hundred and forty delegates representing nineteen states and one territory. About this time the reform which hitherto looked chiefly to the rescue of the inebriate, took a wider scope and a truer method, and began also efforts for the suppression of the traffic in strong drink. In 1836 a second National Convention, presided over by Chancellor Walworth, was held in Saratoga, N. Y. Four hundred delegates attended, and a resolution was adopted that henceforth the pledge should be *total abstinence from all that intoxicates.* The legislative war against the traffic began in 1838. The license laws of several states were made more stringent. Massachusetts passed a law prohibiting the sale of alcoholic liquors in less quantity than fifteen gallons. The agitation spread rapidly, and the irresistable logic by which the enthusiasm of the reformers was supported, gave it a position from which it has never been dislodged. In the year 1840 began the great temperance revival known as the "Washingtonian" movement. In the city of Baltimore six hard drinkers met for a night's carousal; they suddenly resolved to reform, signed a pledge, and formed an organization for active work. They held meetings, recited the simple story of their degradation by strong drink, and of their happy deliverance from the bondage of appetite, and invited those still in the consuming fires of dissipation to join them. They met with a wonderful response, their enthusiasm was communicated to vast assemblies, and went on in eddying currents forming new centres and new lines of aggression. All classes caught the inspiration of the new movement and helped on the good work. It is estimated that in two or three years one hundred and fifty thousand drunkards had signed the pledge, many of whom kept it to the end of life in the vigor of a restored manhood. The whole country was profoundly moved, and new organizations began to spring up, and the reform constantly gained in strength. From this period on to the outbreak of the Civil War, public sentiment grew rapidly, and great progress was made in various lines of effort. The Civil War absorbed the interest of all classes, and diverted thought for a time from this great cause, while it directly aided in many ways the demoralizing influences at work in society. After the war was over these unfavorable influences continued to be felt for several years, but the temperance sentiment soon began to reassert itself, and men began to advocate the abolition of a slavery more terrible than that which went down in the war. A remarkable movement began in 1873 in Ohio among the

Christian women who had long been holding meeting for prayer for the success of the temperance cause. That movement is known as the "Women's Temperance Crusade," and out of it came much of the force now so mighty in all the land in behalf of this cause.

Having given this general outline of the growth of the reformation, let us now look more closely at some of the forces in the field by which it is still being carried forward. This is the most active and aggressive period ever known in temperance work, not only in this country but throughout the world.

First in order of time, and of importance also, we must name THE CHURCH. Its whole spirit and aim, the drift of all its teaching and services, is for the suppression of vice in all forms, the restraint of fleshly indulgences, and the cultivation of all the virtues that enoble man and bless society. The indirect power of the gospel in developing conscience and moral sentiment, and in begetting a better style of life out of which temperance work naturally arises, has furnished the soil for all the harvest that is now being gathered. If the church had never undertaken specific temperance teaching and work, its indirect influence would still make it the most influential factor in the great reformation. Back of Women's Crusades, Temperance Unions and Prohibition movements have been the ministers of the gospel and the mighty host of consecrated laymen, who have given their influence in favor of truth, righteousness and sobriety. Converted, regenerated souls, and those they have influenced, have been the secret springs whence these waters for the life of the nation have issued. But the churches have also been leaders in direct temperance work. THE METHODIST CHURCH in all its branches, inherited from John Wesley, its founder, a positive hostility to strong drink as a beverage, and has been practically a total abstinence society in all its history. Its general rules forbid the use of intoxicating drinks as a beverage, and its discipline prohibits the manufacture or sale of strong drink, or the renting of property for such purposes by any of its members. This places that numerous body of Christians far in advance of any other denomination on this subject. It is also true that in the great popular agitations by which intelligent conviction on the subject has been formed, the ministers of this church have been leaders. With ready access to the great masses of our population, they have everywhere with singular unanimity proclaimed the advanced doctrine of the denomination on this subject, and engrafted upon the religious life this healthy temperance sentiment; it is made a part of the religious life of the denomination, and, therefore, is tenacious and powerful. The ministry is not embarrassed by brewers, distillers, or liquor dealers as trustees or other officials, for the law of the church as well as its prevailing sentiment excludes them. The pulpit is free on this subject, and its freedom has been used with great effect against the evil genius of intemperance. It is impossible to estimate the influence of twenty thousand ministers thus free from all alliances with the evil, and actively engaged in teaching the most exalted sentiments on the subject. In all the states where the question of prohibition has been agitated these men have stood in the front of the battle, giving and receiving the heaviest blows, some of their number falling as martyrs to the cause. In the States of Iowa and Kansas, in both of which the Methodists outnumber all other Protestant Christians combined, the final success of pro-

hibition is by all intelligent observers conceded to be due
in a large degree to their influence.

THE PRESBYTERIAN CHURCH, if less pronounced in its
law and less uniform in its practice, has been a great
power in the temperance reform. Many of its ministers
unfurled the banner of temperance in this country before
our national flag had kissed the breezes. Dr. Rush was
an honored member of that church and appeared before
the General Assembly in a most earnest address in
behalf of the cause to which he contributed so much.
The General Assembly, also the Presbyteries and Syn-
ods, have, at various times, made very strong deliverances on the subject, and the great body of the ministry
has stood in support of the most advanced sentiment
concerning it.

THE BAPTIST CHURCH has contributed many illustri-
ous names to this great reformation. Its spiritual life
and evangelizing efforts, more than any formal church
action on the subject, has given the cause great support.
Its ministers, in large numbers, have been fearless and
faithful advocates of the most advanced views. Its public deliverances in conventions have been strong and
wise, and its publications have been bold and true in
support of the cause.

We might continue the list of churches, giving to each
a well-deserved place of honor in the catalogue of forces
battling against the greatest evil of the age. But what
is said of one may, with slight variations, be said of all,
they belong to the conquering host of God's great army
that is marching to the complete overthrow of the mar-
shalled forces of rum. *The Episcopal, the Congregational,
the Lutheran, the Reformed,* and all the other churches, by
indirect influences and by direct effort in such forms as

seem to them wisest, are helping forward the grand consummation for which all good people are praying, when
"there shall be nothing to hurt or harm in all the holy
mountain of God." All the prayers and services of the sanctuary, whether they make special mention of the evils of
intemperance or not, by all the force with which they are
lifting men to higher and holier lives, are resisting those
evils, and in their final overthrow will be found to have
been one of the most mighty forces in accomplishing
that result. Those who engage in specific temperance
work, in its various departments, here receive much of
their inspiration and strength. They go forth from the
sanctuary renewed, re-consecrated to the good work, with
more faith, a loftier purpose, a purer aim, with moral
ideas clarified, and clad anew in that Divine armor
which makes the true man invincible. Great as are the
reforming influences of the church, the nature of the evil
to be overcome in this contest is such as to justify the
formation of special organizations outside the church for
that purpose. We have in the field a great number of
such organizations doing very effective work against the
prince of darkness.

The oldest of these is the SONS OF TEMPERANCE. It
grew out of the great "Washingtonian" movement, and
was organized in New York in 1842. It was designed to
give permanency and body to that wonderful temperance
revival, to organize its results, and to afford a basis for
still further aggression upon the enemy's territory.
Already the workers in this good cause had seen the sad
effects of reaction after such a great awakening, for the
revival of 1830 was followed by the depression that was
most manifest in 1838. The records of the Washingtonian movement show that their reasoning was correct, for

out of 600,000 drunkards who signed the pledge in that
great revival, 450,000 are said to have returned to their
old ways. The "Sons of Temperance" endeavored to
prevent this outgoing tide by building around these men
the protection of a secret order, specially devoted to the
work of saving men from the evils of intemperance. It
was a great brotherhood into which reformed men might
come for sympathy, encouragement, and help in their
struggle against appetite within and temptation from
without. The unfortunate men who were reclaimed
by the great temperance revival, came up from the
lowest depths of poverty, as well as from the most
loathsome vices, and if they were to be made secure in
their new life, some provision must be made for meeting their necessities and for placing them in positions
for maintaining themselves. This was another strong
reason for the organization of this order, and it did great
service in this direction in helping men to a better financial as well as to a purer moral condition. Many poor
men only half rescued were, by this order, drawn entirely
out of the devouring flames, and became bright orna-
ments to society and pillars in the church. It was a
secret order only in the sense that its meetings were private, which they found a necessary expedient to protect
themselves from being imposed upon by unworthy persons. The growth of the order was very rapid, for it
marched in the wake of the great revival, garnering its
results. In three years time it had gained 40,000 members, and enthusiasm everywhere animated its forces and
added to their numbers. Not only were its numbers
increased, but the sphere of its action was broadened so
as to keep pace with the growing temperance sentiment
of the times. In 1852 it took an advanced position in

declaring for prohibition, and in all subsequent movements it has been a true and staunch ally of the cause.
"During the forty-three years of its existence it has
admitted to membership in America alone, 2,250,000
persons. It has collected for temperance and benevolent
purposes $8,450,000."

Next in order of time comes the TEMPLARS OF HONOR
AND TEMPERANCE." This organization was designed to
supplement the work of the Sons of Temperance, and to
afford some elements of help not found in the older
organization. The enthusiasm of the people was at
white heat, sentiment was growing rapidly, and new
measures were constantly in demand to meet the wants
of the changing conditions. The name "Temple of
Honor," is the embodiment of the great principles which
underlie this order. "What the square and compass are
to the Mason, and the three links are to the Odd Fellow,
what the crescent is to the followers of the prophet, and
the cross to the Christian, the Temple of Honor is to
those who have passed its portals and proven faithful to
its vows." At first it sought an alliance with the Sons
of Temperance as a higher degree in that order, but in
1846 it was decided inexpedient to complete such an
arrangement. The growth of the order was constant
and healthy, though not so rapid as had been that of the
older organization. It is not a political organization,
yet it has constantly aimed at prohibition as the true
goal in all temperance work. It is fraternal in spirit
and aims, seeking to improve men morally, intellectu-
ally and socially, as well as to save them from the evils
of intemperance. It has done a good work, and its
friends expect much from it in the future.

THE CADETS OF TEMPERANCE, an organization for

boys, really began with the Sons of Temperance in 1845. Several attempts were made to so modify the organization of the Sons of Temperance that boys could be admitted, but without success. Finally some boys, after witnessing a parade of one of the Divisions of the Sons of Temperance at Catasaqua, Lehigh Co., Pa., formed an association of their own. Another was soon organized in Bethlehem, Pa., and another in Germantown, Pa. Influential friends took hold of the movement, and it soon spread to Philadelphia and other parts of the State. It has become quite strong also in New York and Maryland and is extending into other States.

Next in the order of time arose the NATIONAL TEMPERANCE SOCIETY AND PUBLICATION HOUSE, organized at a national temperance convention, representing every temperance organization in the country and every religious denomination, held at Saratoga, N. Y., in 1865. For twenty years this society, with head-quarters in New York City, has been doing a great work in creating and disseminating a temperance literature. It now has over 1,400 different publications on the various phases of the temperance question. It also issues the *National Temperance Advocate*, a monthly publication devoted to the temperance reform. It provides liberally for the wants of children, in publications suitable for the Sunday school and the day school. The *Youth's Temperance Banner* is an illustrated four-page monthly, containing a variety of matter well suited to instruct and interest children. It is prosecuting missionary work upon a large scale in needy districts. It sends missionaries and literature among the freedmen of the South, working largely through existing church and educational institutions, and a like service is rendered in hospitals, jails,

14

shops, and other needy localities. It has persistently
labored to secure the appointment by Congress of a
commission of inquiry concerning the traffic in intoxicating liquors and its relation to the public welfare. It
has in many ways contributed to that growth of temperance sentiment, which is one of the marked characteris-
tics of our times.

THE INDEPENDENT ORDER OF GOOD TEMPLARS, one
of the great agencies in the creation of the present sentiment on this subject, arose in central New York in the
summer of 1851. "The order has since spread over all
the civilized world, and now exists in every state and
territory of the United States; in every province of
Canada; in England, Scotland, Wales and Ireland; in
Norway, Sweden and Denmark, and in various other
countries of Europe; in India, China and Japan; in
Africa; in Australia, New Zealand and Tasmania; in the
Sandwich Islands and in many other islands of the
ocean." More than 5,000,000 persons have been
received into the order since it was first established, of
this number it is estimated that 400,000 were hard
drinkers before their reception into the order. The
present membership of the order is over 300,000. The
order enjoins a total abstinence pledge, and many not
now in connection with it hold themselves bound by its
pledge and are faithful to it. It has a sententious put-
ing of its principles that has been the rallying cry in
many a hard fought battle, "*total abstinence for the individual and total prohibition for the state.*" The order is
still vigorous, is doing a good work and gives promise
of great usefulness in the future.

THE NATIONAL PROHIBITION PARTY is a political
organization, designed to secure temperance legislation

by the dominance of a temperance party specially devoted to the work of enacting and enforcing laws against the liquor traffic. It was organized in Chicago in 1869 and has been in the field ever since, at times displaying great vigor. It has proven very influential as an agitator, and has turned attention to the subject in quarters where no other agency seemed to succeed.

THE ROYAL TEMPLARS OF TEMPERANCE came into existence the same year with the prohibition party, but unlike that organization it was not distinctly political in its purposes. Its object was declared to be to "labor unceasingly for the promotion of the cause of temperance, morally, socially, religiously and politically." "No member was eligible to membership who was not at the time of seeking admission a member in good standing of some temperance society or church, or who was not known in the community as an earnest worker in the cause of temperance. Its work was to be educational rather than reformatory, the members preferring to do their reformatory work through other existing organizations." At first limited in its operations to the City of Buffalo, N. Y., it has since extended its operations into a number of states. "It is the rival of no temperance order, but seeks to cheer, encourage and emulate all in their efforts to rid our common country of the evils of intemperance.

THE CATHOLIC TOTAL ABSTINENCE UNION OF AMERICA was organized in Baltimore in 1872. Since the visit of Father Matthew to this country in 1840, who awakened great enthusiasm on the subject wherever he went, and contributed greatly to the rising tide of temperance sentiment in the country, numerous societies have arisen in the Catholic church for the suppression of intemperance. The archbishops and bishops in pastoral letters at various times have warned their people against the pernicious traffic in strong drink, and have urged those engaged in it to abandon it. Temperance sentiment is rapidly growing in that church, and some of the best workers in the cause are of its communion. The numbers of this organization, if not large, are growing, and if true to its obligations and opportunities it has a great future.

One of the most effective of all agencies raised up by Divine Providence for the removal of intemperance and its kindred vices is THE WOMAN'S CHRISTIAN TEMPERANCE UNION, the outgrowth of the great "Crusade" movement which began among the women of Ohio, who were moved as by an irresistible inspiration from heaven. The history of that wonderful uprising has never been written, and the best part of it could not be put on the printed page. When the first storm of enthusiasm had swept by, and the Christian women looked about to see what of a substantial character was left as the result of their toil, they found enough to convince them that the Lord was in the movement, and that they dare not desert it. Then they began to collect their thoughts, and ask how the work might be made permanent and be carried into other states. In the autumn of 1874, they came together from all parts in a convention in Cleveland, Ohio, which continued in session through the 18th, 19th and 20th of November. In this convention the organization took form, and the "Woman's Christian Temperance Union" began its wonderful career. No pen could give an adequate outline of its work, and of the spirit that has actuated it. Ten thousand fountains of pure and living water seem to have broken forth at once in society, diffusing a new spirit and a new life in church, in school, in literature, and in politics. It partakes of the nature of a great social and religious revolution, and if its progress continues, it will doubtless be that in fact in the not distant future. Its indirect influence upon woman's position in society, in church, and even in politics is very great, leading to results that are only as yet partially developed. Its work has so grown that it has been necessary to divide it into several departments, all linked to the great central object, the overthrow of intemperance. Its publication department issues an excellent weekly paper, and has published a great number of books and tracts. Its juvenile department has brought woman's tact and motherly instinct into good and fruitful service among children in the interests of the great reform. The Sunday School department seeks through this arm of the church to reach the young people. The department of scientific instruction has done a great work in securing legislative action in many of the states requiring instruction to be given in the common schools upon the nature of alcohol and its effects on the human system. The department of social purity is doing a greatly needed work in the behalf of fallen woman, and for the suppression of "the social evil." God has put upon the women an anointing for this work of which they give abundant proof, both by the spirit in which they go about their work and in the results that follow.

THE NATIONAL LEAGUE FOR THE SUPPRESSION OF THE LIQUOR TRAFFIC, a non-partisan organization, formed in Boston in 1885, is doing good work for the cause.

THE LAW AND ORDER LEAGUES of the various cities, are entitled to be ranked among our temperance forces, as their object is chiefly to secure the enforcement of laws violated in the interests of and by the liquor traffic. They exist in most of the large cities, a fact that in itself is a standing proof of the lawlessness of this corrupting · traffic. They are of recent origin, the first one having been formed in Chicago, but they have accomplished great good in many cities, and there is a large and inviting field before them for future activity.

These and other forces, and a great multitude of earnest, faithful workers not connected with any formal organizations, working upon different lines, are all helping forward the grand consummation to which we all look—the total prohibition of the liquor traffic. The Mississippi River is formed by a great number of streams flowing into it, many of them, as the Tennessee and the Missouri Rivers, flowing in opposite directions, but when they meet at the great central stream they contribute their floods to it and unite to swell its volume and flow together in the same general course. Among these temperance forces some may seem to be moving in opposite directions, so far as method is concerned, but they all are aiding the great temperance reform, and contribute whatever influence they have to it. With such forces, inspired by a lofty enthusiasm, enobled by unselfish aims, and stimulated by the approval of conscience, we may expect increasing devotion to the work undertaken, and by the Divine blessing, final and complete success.

CHAPTER XIV.

CONCLUSION.

HAS the criminal in the dock anything to say why sentence should not be pronounced upon him? It has been alleged for him, in a general way, that he "is a good creature of God," and ought not, therefore, to be condemned. This is another added to the many falsehoods by which the friends of this monster have sought to shield him from the just indignation of mankind. When God looked out on creation and pronounced it "good" there was no "flowing bowl," nor "tempting decanter," on the face of all the earth. "God made man upright, but they have sought out many inventions," among these inventions none has been a greater offence to God or injury to man than the art of producing alcoholic drinks. They are the product, not of life or the life-giving forces of nature, but of death and of the process of decay, the creature not of God but of death and destruction. Man has learned how to arrest or employ the process of decay, so as to draw off in the form of a liquor its very spirit and essence, with all its power of propagation lodged in the liquor. The diseases which destroy human life have the power of going forth from their victim to those near by in good health, and piercing them with their poisoned arrows that fly on the wings of the wind. All evil seems to have this power of propagation. The surgeon in perfect health, who allows the smallest particle of putrifying matter to enter a cut on his hand, must pay the penalty with his life. A small particle floating in the air from a small-pox patient's room, and taken into the lungs of a healthy man will leave him a loathsome corpse, covered from head to foot with the insignia of its power. The product of death and decay in the form of alcoholic drinks, acts by this same law as a propagation of the process to which it owes its being, as a deadly infection. It is the process of decay drawn off in a convenient form for propagation, and wherever it touches it blights and kills with an energy proportionate to its character. If the decay of grains and fruits is allowed to proceed beyond the liquor producing point from which these alcoholic drinks are derived, this deadly spirit is thrown off in the form of gasses, and we have our malaria, and the poisoned atmosphere that produces a great variety of life-destroying diseases. It is not "a good creature of God," but the spirit of evil, derived from the death and decay of God's good creatures. As well might the Devil assume to be the Son of God, as for alcoholic drinks to pretend to be "a good creature of God." This claim does not shield the monster from impending judgment, but only makes more manifest the essential evil that inheres in his character.

It has also been claimed that this traffic merits forbearance because of the revenue derived from it, by which the expenses of government are met. That the government does derive a large revenue from this source I confess with shame, but that it thereby adds to its wealth I deny. It is the mad man's way of getting rich, to burn up his property for the amusement of bystanders who pay him ten cents on the dollar for his loss. The revenue from the liquor traffic is not ten cents on the dollar of the amount it destroys. This plea, based on revenue value, brings to view a most hideous background of loss, want and suffering that proves a powerful argument against the existence of the traffic. Mr. Gladstone, on receiving a remonstrance from the London brewers against some proposed prohibitory legislation in which the revenue argument was used, said:

"Gentlemen, I cannot permit a question of mere revenue to be considered alongside of a question of morals; but give me a sober population, not wasting their earnings on strong drink, and I will know where to get my revenue." Chief Justice Grier, of the United States Supreme Court, when questioned as to the effect of prohibition, said that, "Even should there be a loss of revenue, the Government would be a thousand-fold the gainer in the health and wealth and happiness of her people."

The revenue derived does not even meet the extra charges for the support of paupers, the conviction and punishment of criminals, and the support of civil and police officers made necessary by the traffic, while through all the land it spreads wasting and destruction.

A great clamor has been raised on the ground of legal right, and on the deeper grounds of justice and "personal liberty." To this plea for the life of the accused the preceding pages give a full response, and we here dismiss it with the remark that it is the natural resort of all criminals when their guilt is beyond question. Crime has no right but the right to be punished, and this is the only remaining right of this monster guilty of untold crimes in all parts of the world.

No one has yet given a good and sufficient reason for the continued existence of the liquor traffic. None of

the reformatory, educational, charitable, or religious
institutions have come forward to ask that its life be
prolonged.   The facts and arguments all seem to be
against it.   The most careful search fails to find one
good reason why the traffic should be spared, while no
mind is broad enough to grasp the full significance of
the valid arguments against it.   We have found it the
chief agent in corrupting the young, in robbing the
home, the school and the church, in supplying the poor-
house, the jail, and the gallows, and in filling the land
with orphans and widows.   We have found it destroying property, corrupting politics, poisoning civilization,
and placing its infernal dynamite beneath the very foun-
dations of the republic.   We have found it striking men
down with the most horrible death known in the annals
of time, without regard to age, position, circumstances,
or previous character, carrying down whole families and
communities in the disgrace of its fallen victim.

The terrible catalogue of its wickedness can never be
adequately expressed in language, and we here pause for
the verdict solicited at the beginning of this treatise.
In the name of God and in behalf of suffering humanity
I ask the cordial consent and enthusiastic co-operation
of the American people in pronouncing the liquor traffic
accursed and forever prohibited from setting foot on free
American soil.

INDEX.

219